HARVEST IN TRANSLATION

# The
# Following Story

# Cees Nooteboom

# The
# Following Story

*Translated from the Dutch by Ina Rilke*

A HARVEST BOOK

A HELEN AND KURT WOLFF BOOK

HARCOURT BRACE & COMPANY

*San Diego   New York   London*

First published in Dutch with the title *Het Volgende Verhaal*
First published in Great Britain in 1994 by
Harvill, an imprint of HarperCollins Publishers

Library of Congress Cataloging-in-Publication Data
Nooteboom, Cees, 1933–
[Volgende verhaal. English]
The following story/Cees Nooteboom;
translated from the Dutch by Ina Rilke.—1st Harvest ed.
p.   cm.—(A Harvest book)
ISBN 0-15-600254-X
I. Rilke, Ina.   II. Title.
PT5881.24.O55V6513   1996
839.3'1364—dc20   95-19627

The text was set in Simoncini Garamond.
Designed by Camilla Filancia
Printed in the United States of America
First Harvest edition 1996      A B C D E

# One

Modesty hesitates to express metaphysical concepts directly; if one tries, one delivers oneself up to jubilant misunderstanding.

—THEODOR ADORNO,
*Notes on Literature,* II,
on the final scene of *Faust*

I HAVE NEVER had an exaggerated interest in my own person, but unfortunately that did not imply I could stop thinking about myself at will, from one moment to the next. And that morning I certainly had something to think about. Another man might have resorted to talk about life and death, but such weighty words do not come easily to my lips, even when there is no one else there, as was then the case.

I had waked up with the ridiculous feeling that I might be dead, but whether I was actually dead, or had been dead, or vice versa, I could not ascertain. Death, I had learned, was nothingness, and if that was the state you were in, as I had also learned, all deliberation ceased. So that was not the state I was in, since I was still full of musings, thoughts, memories. And evidently I was still somewhere: pretty soon it would also become apparent that I could walk, look around, eat (the sweetish mother's-milk-and-honey taste of those little buns the Portuguese have for breakfast lingered in my mouth for hours). And I would be able to pay with real money. This last, as far as I was concerned, was the most convincing evidence of all. You wake up in a room in which you did not go to bed, but your wallet is lying as it should on a chair beside your bed. That I was in Portugal I already knew, though I had gone to bed in Amsterdam as usual, but that there should be Portuguese money in my wallet was something I had not expected.

The room itself was immediately familiar. It was the very room that had been the setting of one of the most important episodes of my life, not that I would really call anything in my life important. But I digress. From my years spent as a teacher I know one has to repeat everything twice over to ensure at least the possibility of creating some order out of what appears to be chaos. Let me go back, then, to the first hour of the morning, the moment that I opened my eyes, which I still possessed. "We will feel the draft blowing through the cracks in the structure of causality," someone once said. Well, that morning it was very drafty indeed around me, although the first thing my eyes lighted upon was a ceiling with the most beautifully solid-looking, regularly spaced beams, the kind of structure that by virtue of its functional purity satisfies a need even the most balanced human being feels when returning from the dark realm of sleep. Those sturdy beams were functional because they supported the floor above, and the structure was pure because of the perfectly equal spacing of the beams. So that should have reassured me, but it didn't at all. First of all they were not my beams, and, second, there were sounds coming from above which were most painful to me in that room, the sounds of human lust. There were two possibilities: either it was not my room or this wasn't me, and in the latter case these were not my eyes or my ears, since not only were these beams narrower than those in my bedroom on the Keizersgracht, but also, and more important, in Amsterdam I had no one living upstairs to importune me with his or her invisible passion. I just lay there motionless, if only to get used to the idea that my eyes were perhaps not my eyes, which is a roundabout way of saying that I lay there mortally quiet because I was scared to death of being someone else.

This is the first time I have tried to tell anyone this, and it isn't easy. I didn't dare move, because if I actually was someone else, I wouldn't know how. Something like that. My eyes, as I shall refer to them for the time being, observed the beams which were not my beams, while the ears, mine or those of my potential other, heard the erotic crescendo above blending with the siren of an ambulance in the street, which wasn't making the proper noises either. I reached to touch my eyes and noticed that they were closed. You can't really touch your eyes: you always lower the blinds first, and the problem then is that you can't see the fingers touching those veiled eyes. Spheres, that was what I could feel. If you are daring, you can even give them a little squeeze. I'm ashamed to say that after all those years on earth I still do not know the exact makeup of the human eye. Cornea, retina, iris and pupil, which double as flowers and students in crossword puzzles, that much I knew, but the actual substance, that vitreous mass of coagulated jelly or gelatine, has always struck fear into me. Whenever I use the word "jelly," everyone invariably laughs, but all the same Cornwall in *King Lear* had cried: "Out, vile jelly!" as he put out Gloucester's eyes, and that is precisely what I had in mind when I squeezed those sightless spheres which either were or were not my eyes.

I lay for some time in the same position, and tried to piece together the events of the previous evening. There was nothing exciting about the evenings spent by a bachelor such as myself, at least not when I was at the center of things. You see that kind of thing sometimes, a dog trying to bite its own tail; a sort of canine tornado is set in motion which comes to rest with the emergence from the storm of the dog as dog. Emptiness, that's what you see in the dog's dizzy eyes, and emptiness was what I felt in that strange bed. Because suppose this were not me, and therefore somebody else (it would be going to far to say *nobody*), it would mean that I would have to think of the other's memories as my own, since everyone calls his memories "my memories."

Self-control is, alas, something I have always had in good measure, or I might have shouted out loud, and whoever the other one was, he was of the same bent, and kept his peace. In short, whoever it was lying there decided to ignore his or my speculations and devote himself to the task of remembering, and since he, whoever it was, referred to himself as "I" in that room in Lisbon, which of course I recognized with devilish precision, I remembered the following: the evening of a bachelor in Amsterdam cooking his own supper, which in my case amounts to opening a can of beans. "You'd eat them cold, straight from the can if you could," an old girlfriend once told me, and she had a point there. The taste is incomparable.

At this point I should, of course, proceed to explain who I am and what I do, but perhaps we'll wait a bit with that. Incidentally, I am a classical scholar, onetime teacher of Latin and Greek, or, as my pupils called me, a dead language teacher. I must have been about thirty at the time. My apartment is filled with books which allow me to live among them. So much for the decor, and that is what the scene must have looked like yesterday: a fairly short man, gingery hair now threatening to turn white, at least if it gets the chance. I tend to behave, so I'm told, like a nineteenth-century English academic. I live on an old chesterfield draped with a well-worn oriental rug to hide the disgorged stuffing, and I read under a standard lamp by the window. I read all the time. The people living across the canal from my house once told me they are always pleased when I am back in Holland, because they regard me as a sort of beacon. The wife even confided that she sometimes observes me through binoculars. "And then when I take another look an hour later, you're still sitting there, in exactly the same position. Sometimes I think you must be dead."

"What you call dead, madam, is in fact concentration," I said, because I have no equal when it comes to cutting short unwanted conversations. But she insisted on knowing what I spent all my time reading. Such moments are quite enjoyable, for this conversation took place in one neighborhood café De Klepel, and I have a powerful, some would even say aggressive, voice. "Last night I was reading Theophrastus's *Characters,* madame, and after that I read some page of Nonnos's *Dionysiaca.*" That sort of remark is guaranteed to bring an instant hush in such surroundings, and from then on I am left in peace.

But now I am talking about a different yesterday evening. I had breezed home on the wings of five gins, and had opened my three cans: Campbell's Mock Turtle, Heinz's Baked Beans in Tomato Sauce, and Heinz's frankfurters. The sensation of the can-opener ripping through metal, the unmistakable *toc* as you pierce the air-tight lid and you get a whiff of the contents, the way it guides itself around the rim and the indescribable sound that goes with it, it is one of the most sensual experiences I know, though in my case that doesn't mean very much. I eat my meals sitting on a kitchen chair at the kitchen table, facing a reproduction of a scene on a dish painted in the sixth century before Christ by Prithinos (who had the impudence to lay claim to the centuries preceding him too): Thetis wrestling with Peleus. I have always had a weakness for the Nereid Thetis, not only because she was Achilles's mother, but principally because, being a daughter of the gods, she resisted marriage to the mortal Peleus. She was right. If one is immortal oneself, the stench emanating from mortals must be intolerable. She tried everything in her power to flee from that future corpse, changing into fire, water, a lion and a serpent in the process. That is the difference between gods and men. Gods can change themselves; humans can only *be changed*. I am very fond of my dish. The combatants avert each other's gaze; only one eye of each is visible, a transverse hole seemingly aimed at nothing. The irate lion crouches by Thetis's strangely elongated hand, the serpent writhes around Peleus's ankles, and yet everything seems transfixed; it is a deathly quiet combat. I always look at that picture when I eat, because I do not allow myself to read during meals too. And I actually enjoy these moments, even if no one will believe me. Cats eat the same food every day, as do lions in the zoo, and I have never heard them complain. Piccalilli on the beans, mustard on the frankfurters, which, now that I hear myself speak, reminds me that my name is Mussert. Herman Mussert, same as our national traitor. Not especially felicitous to share one's name with a quisling—Mustard would have been better—but what can you do. And my voice is powerful enough to stifle the merest snigger.

After supper I washed the dishes and settled down in my armchair with my cup of Nescafé. Lamp switched on, so the neighbors can find their way home. First I read some Tacitus, just to get the better of the gin. It always works. Words of polished marble drive out the most evil fumes. After that I read something about Java, for, since losing my job, I have written travel guides, a moronic activity whereby I earn my living, but not nearly as moronic as all those so-called literary travel writers who can't resist pouring out their precious souls over the landscapes of the entire planet, just to amaze the middle classes.

Then I picked up the evening paper, which contained exactly one item worth cutting out and taking to bed with me, and that was a photograph. The rest was all Dutch politics, and one has to be suffering from softening of the brain to take an interest in that. Then an article about the budget deficit, which I have myself, and a piece about corruption in the Third World, but I had already read all about that in Tacitus—you can check and see: Book II of the *Histories,* chapter LXXXVI, where he deals with

Antonius Primus (*tempore Neronis falsi damnatus*).*
People can't write to save their lives nowadays. No
more can I, nor do I want to, despite the fact that
one out of four Dutchmen owns a travel guide by
my pseudonym Dr. Strabo (the name Mussert having
of course been refused by the publisher). "Leaving
the lovely gardens of the Saihoji temple behind, we
now return to our starting point"—that sort of stuff,
and most of it copied straight from others, too, as
are all cookery books and travel guides. A man must
live. But as soon as I qualify for my pension next
year, it will all be over; then I will get on with my
Ovid translation. "And of Achilles, once so great,
remains but . . . but . . ." That was the point I
had reached last night—*Metamorphoses, Book XII,*
I might add—and then my eyelids started drooping.
The meter wasn't right, and never, as I knew full
well, would I be able to attain the polished simplicity
of *et de tam magno restat Achille nescio quid parvum,
quod non bene compleat urnam.* ". . . scarce enough
to fill an urn . . ." Never will there be another
language like Latin, never again will precision and
beauty and clarity be so epitomized. Our modern
languages are altogether too wordy; look at any
bilingual edition: on the left the spare, measured
Latin phrases, the sculptured lines, on the right the
full page, the traffic jam, the jumble of words,
blathering chaos. No one will ever set eyes on my

* falsely condemned for betrayal in the time of Nero.

translation; if I am to be interred in a grave I will take it with me. I do not wish to join the ranks of the dabblers. I undressed and went to bed, carrying with me the photograph I had cut out of the paper, and lay there mulling it over, dumbly. The photograph had not been taken by a someone, but by a something: a spacecraft, the *Voyager,* at six billion kilometers away from the earth from where it came. That sort of thing does not really impress me. My tiny lifespan, the utter insignificance of my existence, they are no more microscopic for being viewed from such a distance. But I had a special relation to the *Voyager,* because I had the feeling that I had traveled with him myself. Anyone can look this up in Dr. Strabo's *Guide to North America,* although there is no mention of the cheap thrill I felt at the time— that would be preposterous.

I had gone to visit the Air and Space Museum in Washington because my publisher had said that young people were interested in such things. Young people. The very phrase sets my teeth on edge. But I am obedient by nature. Technology means little to me. It is the incessant stretching of physical possibility with unforeseeable consequences. One probably can't become enthusiastic unless one already partly consists of aluminum and plastic oneself, and no longer believes in the existence of free will. But some machines have a beauty of their own—although I would never admit it in public—and so I was reasonably content to be wandering around among the small suspended airplanes dating from modern pre-history, and contemplating the blistered space capsules which offer such a convincing demonstration of our current state of mutation. Obviously space is our destiny, that much I concede. After all I live there myself. But the excitement of the great voyages of discovery will pass me by; I will always belong to those who are left behind on the quay waving good-bye to the departing; I belong to the past, to the time before Armstrong put his big corrugated footstep on the face of the moon. That was another thing I got to see that afternoon, for without thinking anything in particular I had drifted into a sort of theater where there was a film about space travel. I found myself sitting in one of those American swivel chairs that hug you like a womb, and setting off on my journey through space. Almost immediately tears sprang to my eyes. Not a word about anything like that in Dr. Strabo's guidebook, naturally. Emotion ought to be inspired by art, and here I was being misled by reality; some technical wizard had worked optical magic to strew the lunar gravel at our feet, so that it was just as if we ourselves were standing on the moon and walking around. In the distance shone (!) the unimaginable planet Earth. How could there ever have been a Homer or Ovid to write about the fate of gods and men on that ethereal, silvery, floating disc? I could smell the dead dust at my feet, I saw the puffs of moon powder whirl upward and settle again. I was divested of my being, and no substitute was in the offing. Whether the humans all about me were having the same sensation I do not know. It was deathly quiet. We were on the moon and yet we would never get there; in a while we would step outside into the shrill daylight and go our separate ways on a disc no bigger than a guilder, a free-floating object adrift somewhere in the black drapery of space. But things got even worse. I am custodian of the most beautiful texts ever composed on earth—at least that is how I feel—but I have never shed a tear over a single line or figure of speech, as I have never been able to weep over the things that are supposed to make one weep. My tears are triggered only by kitsch. When He sets eyes on Her in full Technicolor, by the schmaltz of plebeian imagination complete with singing strings, perverted honey that is devised to trap the soul, the very idea of music turned against itself. That was the music that was now being played, and my tears were unstoppable. Churchill, they say, cried about everything, but probably not when he gave the order to bomb Dresden. Off went the *Voyager,* a futile, man-made machine, a gleaming spider in empty space, wafting past lifeless planets, where sorrow had never existed except perhaps for the pain of rocks groaning under an unbearable burden of ice, and I wept. The *Voyager* sailed away from us into eternity, emitting a bleep every now and then and taking photographs of all those gelid or fiery but ever lifeless spheres which, together with the orb we must live on, revolve round a flaming bubble of gas; and the amplifiers, placed invisibly around us in the dark theater, sprayed us with sound in a desperate attempt to corrupt the silence of the solitary metallic voyager. A compelling, velvety voice began speaking, at first making itself heard through the music, then as a solo instrument. In ninety thousand years' time, the voice intoned, the *Voyager* would have reached the outer limits of our galaxy. There was a pause, the music swelled like toxic surf, and fell silent again to allow the voice to fire a parting shot: "And then, maybe, we will know the answer to our eternal questions."

The humanoids in the theater cringed.

"Is there anyone out there?"

All around me it was as quiet now as in the deserted streets of the universe across which the *Voyager* hurtled noiselessly, bathed in a cosmic glow, and only in the fifth of its ninety thousand years. Ninety thousand! By that time the ashes of the ashes of our ashes would long since have disowned our provenance. We would have never been there! The music gathered momentum, pus oozed from my eyes. How about that for a metamorphosis! The voice gave forth one final burst: "Are we all alone?"

Suddenly I knew the answer. This voice was not attached to a throat. It was a voice that was already part of our absence, just as the music had been the negation of everything Pythagoras had expressed in his theory of harmony. I shuffled out with all the

15

others, feeling elated and antlike at the same time. In the mirror of the men's room I inspected my absurd red eyes, and I knew that I had not wept over my mortality, but over the falsehood, the fraud. If I had been at home, I would have restored order with a madrigal by Gesualdo (a murderer who wrote the purest music on earth), but here I had to make do with a large bourbon. In the distance, serene and colonial, stood the White House, where without doubt something appalling was being concocted at that very moment.

And now (to use the unspeakable word that always cuts the ground from under one's feet), I was lying in a room in Lisbon with my eyes shut tight, thinking about that other *now* of the previous evening (if it had been the previous evening), when I had lain in bed open-eyed, gazing at the photograph. Just as the mechanical *Voyager* had moved on since then, so had I, I writing my imbecile guides, the *Voyager* taking endless photographs, six of which I now held, grouped together, in my hand: Venus, the planet Earth, Jupiter, Saturn, Uranus, Neptune, all old friends of mine from my hours with Ovid, metamorphosed by now into dingy specks of light on coarse-grained, grimy winding-sheets which undoubtedly represented space. "*Voyager* is now leaving the solar system," the caption read. Bully for him! Off into the wide blue yonder! Leaving us all alone! And then to send home a snapshot that might just as well be of any one of a billion other stars in the backwaters of the universe, for the express purpose of adding to our humiliation, while we had in fact not only made the photographer with our own hands but had also dispatched it on its journey, so that ninety thousand years from now we would at least know more or less where we stood.

I noticed that I was getting drowsy, and at the same time it was as if a great wave swept me up, lifting me, engulfing me, carrying me along with a force that I did not know existed. I thought of death, but it was not because of the wave, it was still because of the photograph. In my case each thought immediately leads to another. I can't help it, and thanks to those pathetic newspaper stars in my hand I saw one of those *Vanitas* paintings which served our forebears as a memento mori: some hermit or other (if there was a cardinal's hat to be seen among the melancholy thistles at his bare feet, it was sure to be St. Jerome) hunched over a table, alternately staring at the skull belonging to someone who never could have been as entertaining as Hamlet's Yorick, and at the tormented figure on the cross. Ominous clouds, barren landscapes, a lion lurking in the shadows. Perhaps they rebelled against the world simply because they were still in possession of it. Ours is a mere photograph in a newspaper, shot from a distance of six billion kilometers. That the newspaper I was holding existed simultaneously on that dingy star was plainly a miracle, but I don't know if such things crossed my mind at the time. Usually I can manage to retrace my thoughts all the way back to that bizarre and degrading moment of falling asleep, when the mind must surrender to the body as it lays itself down at nightfall with the obeisance of servants, desiring nothing but the pretense of absence.

Yesterday it was different. It struck me that the thought preoccupying me, whatever it was, had been trying desperately to attune itself to the slow wave that seemed to be bearing me along. The entire universe was out to anesthetize me, and it was as if I was trying to sing along with that numbing formula, to be part of it, as the fish becomes part of the current by which it is borne. But whatever I wanted to do—fly, swim, sing, think—I couldn't. The mightiest arms in the world had raised me up in Amsterdam, and had apparently put me down again in a room in Lisbon. They had not done me any harm. There was no pain. Nor did I feel—how shall I put it?—regret. And I was not curious, but that may have been thanks to my daily intercourse with Ovid's *Metamorphoses*. See Book XV, verses 60–64. I too have my bible, one that really helps. Furthermore, although I hadn't yet looked in the mirror, my body felt like its familiar self. So I had not turned into someone else; I was merely in a room I could not possibly be in, not if I had any understanding of the rules of logic. And I knew that room, because I had slept there twenty years ago with another man's wife.

The rancidness of that concept brought me back to the world. Indeed, I raised my knees and stuffed the pillow that lay unused next to mine under my head, so that I was half sitting up. There's nothing better than a full-blown déjà vu, and yes, they were still there, the vapid portrait of that overestimated seventeenth-century poet Camões, and the engraving of the great Lisbon earthquake with minute faceless creatures scattering in all directions to escape the toppling buildings. I had even made funny remarks about them to her, but she didn't like such jokes. She was not there for jokes but for revenge, and for that she needed me. Love is the pastime of the bourgeoisie, I had once said, but of course what I meant was the middle classes. And so now I was in love, and thus a member of the same weak, glutinous fraternity of one-track-minded automatons which I had always claimed to despise. I tried to convince myself that it was passion we were engaged in, but if that was true in her case, the passion was certainly not aimed at me, but at her putty-faced husband: a giant built up from slabs of veal, bald, with a permanently set grin, as if he never stopped passing around the biscuits. A teacher of Dutch—well, if you wanted to draw a cartoon of the type, you could take him as your model. Teaching children the language they were already hearing in the echo chamber of the womb long before they were born, and stunting the natural growth of that language with tedious drivel about ordinal numbers, double possessives, split infinitives, predicate nouns and prepositional phrases is bad enough, but to look like an underdone cutlet and pontificate about poetry, that's too much. And not only did he lay down the law about poetry, he wrote it too. Every few years he would spawn yet another anemic assembly of messages from the lukewarm provinces of his soul: toothless lines, strings of words casting aimlessly about on the page. If they ever happened to brush against a single line of Horace, they would disintegrate without a trace.

I sat up straight and felt a pressing urge to see myself, not because of what I would see, for I hated my appearance, and for good reason. No; it was the confrontation I was after. I had to know which version of me was here in that room of the past, the current version or the former one. I didn't know which was worse. I stuck one leg out of the bed, a pale old-man's leg. But that was what my legs had always looked like, so that was no help. There was only one solution: the mirror in the bathroom, and I got out of bed to take a look without the hesitation one might expect after all those years. Well, there I stood. I don't know whether I was relieved to find that I did not necessarily have to be my former self, and that the man standing there bore more than a passing resemblance to the man whose features I had not been able to elude in my Amsterdam mirror the night before. "Socrates," that was my nickname at the provincial grammar school where I had taught, and it was apt, for that was what I looked like. Socrates without beard, and with glasses, that same face flung together with misshapen blobs of clay, which would never suggest the idea of philosophy in anyone unless they happened to know what manner of words had flowed from those sagging lips under the blunt nose with flared nostrils, and what manner of ideas had taken shape behind that street-fighter's forehead. Without my glasses, as I was at that moment, it had been even worse.

"The spitting image of Socrates" was what she had said the first time she asked me to take off my glasses. Whenever I do that I feel like a tortoise without a shell. That is to say, in the intimate proximity of a female body I am the most defenseless of creatures. Which explains why I have kept largely aloof from those activities which everyone is always going on about and which, to me, have more to do with the animal kingdom than with human beings who concern themselves with the less tangible aspects of existence. Indeed it was the touching in such situations that let me down. My touching was more like the pawing and clawing of a blind man, for although I was perfectly aware of roughly where my hands were supposed to go, my eyes refused point-blank all cooperation upon the removal of the two circular slaves that were my glasses. All I could see, if you could call that seeing, was a more or less pink mass with what appeared to be a random protuberance here and there or a dark spot. What irritated me most of all was that my innocent hands, which in these mercifully rare instances were only trying to help, would promptly be accused of being rough, uncouth, clumsy, as if my fingers were a bunch of child molesters on the run from an institution. But I don't want to enlarge upon the curious details that love between human beings entails. Suffice it to say that she was doing her very best. That is another thing I have learned: when women are out to get something, they are capable of mobilizing forces that men, for all their so-called strength of purpose, cannot match. I looked at me. The yellow lamplight of the past had been replaced by neon, which gives even the most handsome features the pallor of a corpse. But that was not what I saw before me. It was more that now (that word again) I had truly turned into Socrates. Beard, glasses, the attributes no longer mattered. The man standing there, the one I had never loved, invoked my love. But why? That ruffian's face had accompanied me all my life, but there was something extra now, something I could not put my finger on. What was the matter with me? Something had happened to me and I did not know what it was, something compared to which my unexpected presence here was an insignificant detail. I stuck out my tongue, as I do quite frequently. In all its porcine simplicity it is still one of my most attractive features, and when I stick it out to myself in the mirror, nine times out of ten it helps me enormously to concentrate. Call it a form of meditation, if you like, which brings me straight back to an earlier thought. And suddenly I knew what I had been thinking the previous evening, if it had been the previous evening. The wave that had overwhelmed me in my sleep or half-sleep had been fear, physical fear that I would fall off the earth which hung there, so detached and unprotected in space. I tried to conjure up the same fear again, but it did not work. Armed with all Newton's laws I stood there, glued to the red tiles in the bathroom of room 6 of the Essex House in Lisbon, and I thought of Maria Zeinstra, biology teacher at the school where her husband, Arend Herfst, also taught. And where I too taught, of course. While she explained the workings of the human memory and how animals die, I, separated from her by a mere ten centimeters of brick wall, talked about gods and heroes and the ambushes of the aorist, and the greasy titters of puberty welled up from the classroom on the other side, where he was teaching; as usual he was fooling around, dealing with nothing at all, which accounted for his enormous popularity. A living poet, and coach of the basketball team to boot! Rather different from a stunted Socrates with nothing to offer except a pile of two-thousand-year-old corpses, who had buried the treasure of their language so successfully under the covers of a hermetic syntax as to be inaccessible to the admirers of living classics such as Prince, Gullit and Madonna. But once in a while, a very long while, in a rare year of grace, one pupil comes along to make you forget the penetrating odor of unwillingness and aversion, someone who joins you on the delicious surf of the hexameter, someone with an ear for music, who soars effortlessly over the hurdles of case endings, who follows the train of thought, sees the connections, the structure, the beauty. That word again, but it cannot be helped. I was ugly and beauty was my passion—not the visible, immediately tangible kind, but the other, far more mysterious variety hiding behind the defenses of a dead language. Dead! If those languages were dead, then I was Christ and able to raise Lazarus. And in that one year of grace there was someone who actually understood. No, it was worse; she had the same ability. She lacked the knowledge I had, but that didn't matter. Every line of Latin that Lisa d'India bent over began to flower, to live, to stream. She was a miracle, and although I still do not know why I am here, I know she has something to do with it.

I am going back a little, but the strangeness remains, as if I had an inner glow. If I was afraid last night, now I am moved. Essex House—silly name for a Portuguese hotel—in the Rua das Janelas Verdes, close to the Tagus. "Within my being I'm decaying, I know now the cause of my dying, on the banks of the Tagus' flow, where life is light and slow"—Slauerhoff. I remember one day in class talking about the sinister role of the preposition *aan* in that line. We don't die *of* things but *on* things, so only in Dutch can you die on cancer and on the Tagus, but no one laughed, except her. I must get out of this bathroom; my own presence is becoming oppressive. I wonder if I am hungry, and I think not. I ring room service for breakfast. "Pequeno almoço," I had forgotten I could speak Portuguese. The voice at the other end is quiet, friendly, young. A woman. No trace of surprise, nor from the girl delivering my breakfast. Or am I mistaken, is there is a new touch of respect in her behavior, a respectfulness (ludicrous word, really) that I have learned not to expect from servants nowadays? I sit down on the floor, cross-legged, and spread the breakfast things around me. All right, I know, I must settle down to the business of memory. The room insists. I have exactly the same feeling I used to have when contemplating a pile of Herodotus translations that needed correcting. I have long had a weakness for that transparent fabulist, since invented history is always more appealing than the wearisome tyranny of fact. But the prospect of witnessing how my pupils butchered the old liar's admittedly less than pristine prose was enough to put anyone off. Except when there was a translation of hers in the pile, if only because she would sometimes add details entirely of her own invention: a Persian custom, a Lydián princess, and Egyptian god.

I was the only one in the entire school, from the headmaster, teachers male and female, down to the caretaker, who was not in love with Lisa d'India. Not just in my subject was she good, she was good in all subjects. In math she was clarity, in science the spirit of adventure, while in languages she entered into the very soul of the language. Her first stories were published in the school magazine, and they were the stories of a woman among the stories of children. The winning point that had secured our team the basketball tournament had been scored by her. Physical beauty, on top of all this, was certainly superfluous, but it was undeniable: among the sixty eyes in a classroom, hers were impossible to avoid. She had white streaks in her black hair, as if she had already had a long life behind her, the token of a different temporal order in the domain of youth. Perhaps her body knew that she must die young. I called her Graea to myself, after the daughters of Keto and Phorkys, who were white-haired from birth and infected with a dreadful antiquity. One day I mentioned this to her, and she looked straight through me, as people do when their thoughts are elsewhere, or when something you said has reached a secret compartment of their psyche, something they already know but do not want to share with others. She was the daughter of Italian immigrants who, together with the early contingents of Turkish, Spanish and Portuguese guest-workers, undertook to unlock the Netherlands from their centuries-old provincialism. If her father, a steelworker from Catania, had known of her affair with Arend Herfst, he would probably have killed him outright, or would at the very least have raised hell with the headmaster, who was having a hard enough time because he himself had had to surrender Lisa to the detestable Herfst. Why those things had not come out in the open earlier I don't know; it was as if everyone, teachers and pupils, had woven a veil of silence around her, perhaps because we all knew that silence would do the trick, that it would make her disappear. And we included me. But I was not in love with her, I could not fall in love with her. My categorical imperative is very firmly anchored in my system: falling in love is prohibited; therefore I am incapable of it. For the few years that she was my pupil I experienced a form of happiness that has to do with love, but not with the vulgar sort of love that radiates from the ubiquitous TV screen, nor with the embarrassing, banal and uncontrollable affliction known as "being in love." I knew more than enough about the attendant miseries. Now for once in my life I belonged to the ranks of ordinary people, the mortals, the rest, because I was in love with Maria Zeinstra. One single time, and fate struck right away.

I'm glad the others have gone and that I need tell only you my story, even though you yourself are in it. But you already know that, and I have left you as you are. Third person singular, until I can't take it any more. *Banalitas banalitatis.* That was the formula I used for twenty years to exorcise even the faintest evocation of the events of those days. As far as I'm concerned I had drunk from the waters of Lethe: the past did not exist; there was just a succession of hotels with two, three or five stars and the drivel I wrote about them. So-called real life had only once interfered with me, and it had been a far cry from what the words, lines, books had prepared me for. Fate had to do with blind seers, oracles, choruses announcing death, not with panting next to the refrigerator, fumbling with condoms, waiting in a Honda parked around the corner and surreptitious encounters in a Lisbon hotel. Only the written word exists; everything one must do oneself is without form, subject to contingency without rhyme or reason. It takes too long. And if it ends badly the meter isn't right, and there's no way to cross things out. So write, Socrates! But no, not him, and not me either. To write when so much has been written is the preserve of the presumptuous, the blind, those who cannot taste their own mortality.

At this point I would like to be still, to wash away all those words. You have not told me how much time I have for my story. I have lost all sense of measure. I would like to hear a madrigal right now, by Sigismundo d'India. Clarity, timing, only voices, the chaos of sentiments tamed by the perfect structure of the composition. It was in my house that she first heard a madrigal by d'India. "Your ancestor," I said, as if offering her a gift. Fool that I am. And always have been. The caste-less teacher beside the royal pupil. She was standing in front of my bookcase, my only true family tree, her wonderfully long fingers approaching Hesiod and Horace, when she turned and said: "My dad's a steelworker," as if she wanted to make the distance between herself and the music as vast as possible. But I was not in love with her; I was in love with Maria Zeinstra.

I must get out of this room! Which room? This one here, this room in Lisbon. Socrates is scared, Dr. Strabo doesn't dare show his face, Herman Mussert doesn't know whether he has been registered at the reception desk. "Who's that funny-looking guy?" "Which room is he in?" "Have you entered his name?"

Nothing of the sort happens. I gather up my green Michelin, my map of Lisbon. Everything was to hand, naturally. Traveler's checks, escudos in my wallet; someone loves me, *ipsa sibi virtus praemium.** And the fear was unfounded, for the radiant nymph

* virtue is its own reward.

to whom I give my key envelops me with the brilliance of her eyes and says: "Bom dia, Doctor Mussert." August, the imperial month. The pale blue remnants of the wisteria, the shaded patio, the stone steps descending, the same doorman stewed in twenty years of slowly passing time. I recognize him, he acts as if he recognizes me. I must turn left, to the small pastelaria where she used to gorge herself on little brioches the color of egg yolk, the honey varnishing her eager lips. The pastelaria is still there; the world is everlasting.

"Bom dia!" I eat one of those cakes in her honor, just to savor once more the taste of her mouth. A cafézinho, strong, bitter: my own contribution. Filled with bittersweetness I cross the street to the kiosk to buy the *Diário de Notícias,* but the world news is not for me. Nor was it then, incidentally. Today it's Iraq, what it was then I don't remember. And Iraq is a belated mask for my own Babylon, for Akkad and Sumer and the land of the Chaldees. Ur, the Tigris and Euphrates, and splendid Babylon, the bordello of the one hundred tongues. I realize that I am humming an old melody, that my step is as sprightly as on my best days. I walk to the Largo dos Santos, then to the Avenida 24 de Julho. On my right I see the little train and the toy trams in their crude colors. Farther down, in the distance, must be my river. Why of all rivers it was the Tagus that moved me most, I did not know. It must have been that first vision, so long ago already, in 1954, when Lisbon was still the metropolis of a decaying empire. We had already lost Indonesia and the British had lost India, but here, along this river, the laws of the real world did not seem to count. The Portuguese still had Timor, and Goa, Macao, Angola, Mozambique—their sun had not yet set, their empire was still so vast as to accommodate day as well as night, so it seemed as if the people I saw in broad daylight were captives in the domain of sleep. Men wearing shoes of a type never seen in the North strolled arm in arm along the wide brown river and conversed in gently drawling latin tongues which, I thought, had something to do with water, the water of tears and the water of oceans, from the Manueline knots decorating the buildings of the former kings to the busy little boats plying between Cacilhas and Barreiro, and the somber farewell salute of the Torre de Belém—the last the departing explorers saw of their fatherland, and the first landmark they would set eyes on when they returned years later. If they ever returned. I had returned, I had walked past the pathetic statue of the Duque de Terceira, who had liberated Lisbon from something or other in the last century, I had crossed the Cais do Sodré dodging the trams, and now I was standing by the river, the same as ever, only I knew it better now. I had seen its source in a green Spanish meadow in the environs of Cuenca, I knew the rock walls it had carved out in Toledo, its wider, slower course across Extremadura, I knew its origins, I could hear the gurgle of water in the language around me. Later (much later) I had told Lisa d'India: "Latin is the essence, French the idea, Spanish the fire, Italian the air [naturally I had said *aether*], Catalan the earth, and Portuguese is water." She had laughed, a clear, high-pitched laugh, but Maria Zeinstra had not laughed. Perhaps I was standing on the very same spot where I had tried it out on her, but she had not been impressed. "Portuguese is rather like whispering, I find," she said, "I can't understand a word. And about the water and so on, that strikes me as a bit gratuitous, doesn't it you? Not very scientific, anyway." As so often, I could not think of anything to say in return. I was grateful for her company, even though my river was too brown for her liking. "You can imagine all that's been dumped into it."

I turn around to face the city rising gradually before me and I know that I am searching for something, but what? Something I want to see again, and I will only recognize what it is when I see it. And suddenly there it is: that absurd little building with the huge clock, a stone structure consisting almost entirely of clock, huge, round, white, with mighty hands in supreme command of time. HORA LEGAL is written in large letters above it, and in the frayed sprawl of the square it actually sounds like a legal text: "Whosoever attempts to interfere with time, wheresoever that may be, whosoever seeks to stretch it, retard it, channel it, stem its flow, divert it, should know that my law is absolute, that my magisterial hands indicate the ephemeral, nonexistent *now,* as they always do. They stand aloof from corrupting division, from the mercenary now of the scholar; mine is the only true now, the durable now encompassing sixty counted seconds"—and now, as then, I stand there and count and look at the great iron hand pointing down to the white, segmented plane between the 10 and the 15 until, with a shudder, it moves to the next vacant lot and commands, decrees, proclaims that that is where now rules now. Now?

A pigeon perched briefly on the arch over the — clock, as if it wanted to make a point, but I had no intention of being distracted from my musings. Clocks served two purposes, in my opinion. The first was to tell people the time, and the second to impress upon me that time is an enigma, an intractable measureless phenomenon into which, out of sheer helplessness, we have introduced a semblance of order. "Time is the system that must prevent everything from happening at once." I had caught that sentence in midair, so to speak, coming from the radio one day. "Was," "had," what am I saying? I am standing here now, and this is where I once stood with Maria Zeinstra, who turned her green North Holland eyes on me and said: "But what are you going on about, meatball? If you can't keep separate the time of science and the time of your poor little heart, you must be in bad shape."

I had not responded, not because I was offended, for I enjoyed being called meatball by her (or lamp-shade, or fried fish, or melonhead, for that matter), but because the answer was waiting for us a hundred meters down the street, on the wall of the British Bar. She had suspected nothing when we went inside, but once we were sitting in the cool shade and she took a first sip of her Madeira I asked: "D'you know what time it is?"

She glanced up at the big wood-framed clock on the wall opposite, and her face immediately assumed the irritated expression of those who hate to see their holy pacts with the regular universe broken. "All right, all right," she said, and looked at her watch. "I get it. Very funny."

"Oh, well, it's just another way to perceive time," I said. "Einstein turned it into molasses, and Dali melted it, watch and all." The clock on the wall had the conventional sequence of figures, to guide us in a more or less orderly fashion through the segment of the great air balloon that has been assigned to us, but the order had been reversed: twenty past six had become twenty to six. It had a dizzying effect on the viewer. I had once asked the proprietor what the origin of the clock was, and he had told me that it had come with the fixtures. And no, he had never seen anything like it either.

"What can you expect from people who drive on the wrong side of the road?" she said. "When shall we go up into the city?"

Subject closed, and I followed the sweep of her red hair up the Avenida das Naus, the avenue of the ships, as if it was not I showing her the city, but she me. That was then, not now. The back-to-front clock is still hanging there—and since I included it in Dr. Strabo's *Travel Guide for Portugal* half the population of Holland has been to see it. Ninety-one correspondents have so far explained to me that you can tell the proper time on the clock by looking in the mirror. Only they didn't add "meatball."

She danced off in front of me like a ship; every male in sight turned to take another look, to see that swaying wonder from the back as well, not because she was so beautiful, but because she, certainly there and at that time, embodied a provocative freedom. There is no better way to say it: it was as if she steered her body through the crowd for the very purpose of being admired by one and all. I had once told her, echoing the famous poem by Roland Holst: "You don't walk like the woman who could never die, but like a woman everyone abandons everything for," and for a moment I thought she was angry, but she merely retorted, "Everyone, that is, except Arend Herfst."

What was it that I always told my class? Purely as *form* Tacitus' *Histories* are annalistic (yes, you oaf, that means in the form of annals and not what you think), but he frequently interrupts his narrative in order to stick with the strict order of events. Perhaps I should do the same: buy a sun hat, get my head together, keep past and present apart, go up the hill, flee the tortuous labyrinth of the Alfama, rest for a while in the cool shade of a *bela sombra* by the Castelo de São Jorge, contemplate the city lying at my feet, survey the state of my life, reverse the order of the clock and make the past run toward me like an obedient dog. I would, as usual, have to do everything myself, and I might as well start right away. But first a sun hat. White, woven straw. It made me considerably taller. "Hey, guys, Socrates is wearing a queer's hat on his specs."

Of all the minds corrupted by the swinging sixties, our headmaster's was the most severely affected. If he'd had his way, we would have been getting tuition from the pupils. One of his choicest inventions was that staff could sit in on each other's lessons. The few who sampled my classes did not come back for more, and I myself tried only two. First I joined the optional religious-instruction class, which was attended by only three pupils and in the course of which the good Doctor of Divinity was alienated from the Christian love-thy-neighbor principle once and for all. The other lesson had to be hers, of course. Why? Because she had never deigned to look at me in the staff room. Why? Because I dreamed of her at night such dreams as I had not dreamed since adolescence, and because Lisa d'India told me what a *fantastic* teacher she was.

And it was true. I had found a seat at the back of the classroom, much to the embarrassment of the gawky teenager next to me, but *she* pretended not to notice my presence. I had asked her if it was all right, and she had said: "I can't stop you, and who knows, it may do you some good: I'm going to talk about death," and that was curiously inaccurate for someone with scientific aspirations, because her lesson was not so much about death as about what comes after, about metamorphosis. And although hers was of a different order than mine, the subject of metamorphosis was familiar to me. It was many years since I had sat at a schooldesk, and because of the reversal of the habitual roles I suddenly saw what a peculiar profession teaching really is. Twenty or more people are sitting down, just one stands; and the knowledge of the one on his feet is somehow supposed to be transmitted to the still-empty brains of all the rest.

She looked good, her red hair waving like a flag through the classroom, but my enjoyment of the spectacle was soon cut short by a screen being unrolled in front of the blackboard and the nonde-script beige curtains being drawn. "Mr. Mussert is a lucky man," she said. "His very first lesson and right off he gets to see a film!" Jeers all around.

"Keep your hands to yourself, Socrates," I heard someone say in the dark, and then it grew quiet, and a dead rat appeared on the screen. It wasn't a big rat, but it was extremely dead—mouth slightly open, some blood on its whiskers, a final glint from a half-closed eye. The broken body lay somewhat arched, in the pose that bears the irreversible mark of death, of arrested motion, of the inability to move ever again. Someone made retching sounds.

"No need for that." It was her voice, short, almost like the crack of a whip. It was quiet at once. Then a sexton beetle appeared on the screen. Not that I knew that that was what it was, but she said so. A sexton beetle, wearing the flaming colors of a fire salamander. I saw a noble creature, ebony and deep ocher, with what looked like escutcheons on its cuirass. Or, rather, her cuirass.

"This is the female."

That had to be true, because it was she who said it. I tried to envisage what this meant. Someone else was doing the same, for a voice said: "Nice bit of stuff!" No one laughed.

The beetle started digging a miniature trench all around the dead rat. A second beetle came along, but it was far less active.

"The male of the species." It would be.

The female began to push against the stiff, un-yielding corpse, shifting it very slightly with each nudge. The dead do not wish to be disturbed, whoever they are. The beetle seemed to want to bend the rat's rigid body: the thick, armored, gleam-ing black head battered repeatedly against the ca-daver, a sculptor working on an outsize block of marble. The image on the screen jumped from time to time, indicating breaks in continuity.

"The film has been edited, as you can see. The whole process was recorded. In all, it takes about eight hours."

The abbreviated version was pretty long, too. The corpse grew rounder, the legs became tangled, the rat's head was pushed deep into its soft belly, the beetle danced its *danse macabre* around a furry ball.

"This is what we call the carrion pellet."

Carrion pellet. I tasted the phrase. Never heard it before. I am always grateful for additions to my vocabulary. And it was an interesting one. A furry ball of rat flesh, slowly rolling into the trench.

"Now she is going to mate with the male in the grave." Someone smacked his lips in the half-light. She switched on the light and turned her gaze on a big, spotty boy in the third row.

"Don't act so shuttered," she said.

Shuttered. What a word! Said in the flat North Holland way. The light was turned off again, but I knew then that the vague emotion she'd already invoked in me had suddenly been promoted to love. *Don't act so shuttered.* The two beetles scurried around to get on top of each other as though under orders, which of course they were. We are the only species that has strayed from that purpose. The same awkward bungling as ever, odder still because most animals don't tend to lie down for it. The antics on the screen had something of an informal dance with one partner having to shove the other around, all in complete silence. A dance without music (the grating of those carapaces must make a deafening noise). But possibly beetles don't have ears; I forgot to ask her about that. The two tanks fell apart and one starting pursuing the other. I had lost track of which was which. She hadn't.

"Now the female is driving the male out of the grave."

The classroom buzzed, the girls making high-pitched sounds. In the midst of it all I could hear her low, conspiratorial laugh, and I felt insulted.

The female started digging a second trench. "For the egg chambers." Again such a novel term. This woman was teaching me new words! There was no doubt about it, I loved her.

"In two days' time she will lay her eggs there. But first she is going to tenderize the carrion."

Her eggs! I had never seen a beetle vomit before. I was sitting in the classroom with the woman I loved and I watched as the science-fiction head of a beetle, magnified a hundred times, vomited green bile over a pellet of carrion that had resembled a dead rat less than an hour ago.

"Now she is gnawing a hole in the carcass." And so she was. The excavator, mother, egg-bearer, lover, murderess, *mamma,* chewed a lump out of the ball of rat and regurgitated it into the hole she had extracted it from. "Now she's making a food trough." Carrion pellet, egg chamber, food trough. And the acceleration of time: in two days the eggs, five days later the larvae. No, I know time cannot be speeded up. Or can it? The eggs are pale and gleaming, seed-colored capsules, the larvae more gently ringed, the color of living ivory. Mother takes a bit of puréed rat, the larvae lick the inside of her mouth. Everything is connected with love. Five hours later they are eating by themselves, the next day they are crawling around in the rolled-up cadaver. *CAro DAta VERmibus:* flesh given to worms. Latin scholar's little joke; sorry. The light was turned on again, the curtains opened, but what was really turned on was her hair. Outside, the sun was shining, the branches of the chestnut tree swayed in the wind. It was spring, but the notion of death had slipped into the classroom, the link between killing, mating, eating, changing—the voracious, serrated chain that is life. The class melted out of the room, leaving the pair of us standing rather awkwardly face to face.

"Next week, mites and maggots."

She said it provocatively, as if she could tell that I was a bit taken aback. Everything I had seen seemed in some way or other to have to do with rage. Rage, or volition. Those grinding mandibles, the medieval stamping of those mating carapaces, the gleaming, blind masks of the larvae licking food out of the armored mouth of their mother—life in the raw.

"The never-ending story," I said. Well done, Socrates, any other great ideas lately?

She puffed up her cheeks. She did that when she was thinking.

"I don't know about that. There's sure to be an end at some point. There has to be a beginning, too." Again that provocative look, as if she had just invented the notion of transience and now wanted to try it out on a scholar. But I was not going to be driven out of the grave that easily.

"Do you want to be cremated?" I asked. That question works wonders in any company. The addressee is reduced to a mere physical encumbrance which must at some point be disposed of. That has a certain piquancy, especially in erotic situations.

"How do you mean?" she said.

"A forensic pathologist once told me that it hurts."

"Nonsense. Well, I suppose there's the possibility of some local sensation."

"Local?"

"Well, when you burn a whole match it curls up, which obviously creates enormous tension in the material."

"I saw a public cremation in Nepal once, on a riverbank." I was lying, I had only read about it, but I could envisage the pyre.

"Oh. And what happened?"

"The skull exploded. An insane sound. As if they were roasting a huge chestnut."

She laughed, and then she stiffened. Outside in the playground—do they still call it that?—Arend Herfst and Lisa d'India strolled by, wearing tracksuits. That was legitimate: he was the team coach. Herfst was on his best behavior. With his set grin, the poet took on something of the larvae I had just seen.

"Is she a pupil of yours?" Maria Zeinstra asked.

"Yes."

"What do you think of her?"

"She is the joy of my old age." I was over thirty, and said this without any irony. Neither of us looked at him; we just watched how the woman beside him redefined the space outside, how the center of the playground shifted as she walked.

"Have you fallen for her, too?" It was intended to sound mocking.

"No." It was the truth. As I have already explained.

"Can I sit in on one of your classes next week?"

"I'm afraid you won't enjoy it."

"Let me be the judge of that."

I looked at her. Green eyes half hidden by her red hair, a bouncy curtain. A galaxy of freckles.

"Why don't you join my Ovid class. I'll be dealing with change, too. Not rats into pellets of carrion, but still . . ."

What should I read that afternoon? About Phaethon and half the globe being consumed by fire? About the dark recesses of the underworld? I tried to imagine how she would sit in my classroom, but I could not.

"Well, see you then," she said, and off she went. When I entered the staff room sometime later, I saw that she was in the middle of having an argument with her husband. His fixed grin had taken on something of a sneer now, and for the first time I saw that she was vulnerable.

You ought to change out of your tracksuit before getting into tragic discussions, I wanted to tell him, but I never say what I think.

Life's a bucket of shit that keeps being added to, and we have to drag it around with us till the end. St. Augustine is supposed to have enunciated this; unfortunately, I never looked up the Latin text. If it is not apocryphal, it is sure to be in the *Confessions*. I should have forgotten all about her by now, it is all so long ago. Grief is supposed to be etched into your face, not into your memory. Besides, it is old-fashioned, grief. It is seldom talked about nowadays. Bourgeois, too. Haven't grieved in twenty years.

It is cool up here in the park. I followed a white peacock (why isn't there a special word for *all* white animals?) as if my life depended on it, and now I am sitting on the wall of the castle, looking out over the city, the river, the dish of sea beyond. Oleander, frangipani, laurel, great elm trees. A girl is sitting nearby, writing. The word "good-bye" is drifting in the air around me and I can't seem to catch hold of it. This entire city is a good-bye. The fringe of Europe, the last shore of the first world, it is there that the corroded continent sinks into the sea, dissolves into the infinite mist which the ocean resembles today. This city does not belong to the present; it is earlier here because it is later. The banal now has not yet arrived; Lisbon is reluctant. That must be the word. This city puts off the moment of parting; this is where Europe says good-bye to itself. Lethargic songs, gentle decay, great beauty. Memory, postponement of metamorphosis. Not one of those things would find its way into Dr. Strabo's *Travel Guide.* I send the fools to the fado taverns, for their dose of processed *saudade.* Slauerhoff and Pessoa I keep to myself, although I do mention them; I direct the poor sods to the Mouraria and to the Brasileira for a cup of coffee, and for the rest I'd sooner keep my mouth shut. I won't breathe a word about the soul-changes of the alcoholic poet, the liquid, multiformed persona who still roams the streets of Lisbon in all his somber brilliance, who has insinuated himself invisibly into tobacconists, quaysides, walls, dark cafés where Slauerhoff and he could easily have been together, unknowing.

The liquid I. The subject had arisen after that first and only time she came to my class. She wasn't having any of it, and I can never explain exactly what I mean. *Regio Solis erat sublimibus alta columnis . . . Metamorphoses,* Book II—that was how I had started my lesson. Maria Zeinstra had sat there watching me, while d'India translated in her high, clear voice: "The palace of the Sun was a tall building with tall columns . . ." and I had said that I preferred "lofty" to "tall," and that it was better anyway not to use the same word twice, and she had bitten her lip hard, as if to draw blood, and had repeated: "The palace of the Sun was a lofty building with tall columns . . ." and only afterward had I got it into my thick Socratic noddle that I was the only one still in the dark about the affair, and that d'India knew that Zeinstra knew and that Zeinstra knew that d'India knew she knew, and all the while I ranted on about the *fastigia summa* and Triton and Proteus, and about Phaethon slowly climbing the steep path to the palace and having to keep his distance from his father because he could not bear the searing light of the Sun God. Oblivious to the third-rate theatricals in the rows in front of me, I was going on about Phaethon's destiny. Regret? No! None? Any idiot would have seen the fear in d'India's eyes, and of course I can still see her before me, the eyes of a wounded deer, her voice clear as always, but much softer than usual. Only, behind her eyes I saw other eyes, and it was to them that I spoke of the son of the god who sought to encircle the earth in his father's chariot. It is obvious from the start that disaster will befall him, that Apollo's foolish son will come crashing down with his golden chariot and fire-breathing horses. I leapt to and fro in front of the class like a whirling dervish; this was my star performance. The purple gates of Aurora flew open to admit the doomed youth with his horses under their jewel-studded yoke, the misguided progeny charging headlong to his rendezvous with death. His downfall would be retold a million times in those hexameters, but I was blind to the live television drama unfolding before my eyes and certainly to the role that *I* might play in it. It was I in that gold-and-silver chariot sparkling with precious stones, I held the reins of the indomitable double span riding across the five zones of heaven. What had my father the Sun said? Not too high or you will set fire to the dome of heaven, not too low or you will scorch the earth . . . But I am off already, I charge through air ringing with joyful whinnies, I see the hooves kicking up a storm as they slice through the clouds like knives, and then it is all over. The chariot hurtles across the sky, spinning out of its eternal orbit, the light refracting in all directions, horses clawing the air, the heat singeing the hide of the Great Bear. I feel how the darkness draws me downward, I know I shall crash; countries, mountains, everything shoots past me in a bolt of confusion; my flames set forests ablaze. I see the poisonous black sweat of the gigantic Scorpion as it raises its tail to sting me; the earth catches fire, the meadows burn to white ashes, Mount Etna spits fire back at me, the ice melts on mountaintops, rivers boil over their banks. I pull the vulnerable world with me in my fate, the incandescent chariot searing my body; the Babylonian Euphrates is alight, the Nile flees in mortal terror and hides its source, all existence laments, and then Jupiter hurls his lethal bolt of lightning, which bores right through me, burning me and dashing me out of the chariot of life; the horses break free and I am flung like a blazing star to earth, my body imploding in a hissing stream, my corpse like a charred rock in the water . . .

Suddenly I notice how quiet it is in the classroom. They stare at me as if they have never seen me before, and to regain my composure I turn my back on all those eyes, green ones too, and write on the blackboard, as if it were not also written in the books in front of them:

HIC · SITUS · EST · PHAETHON · CURRUS
AURIGA · PATERNI
QUEM · SI · NON · TENUIT · MAGNIS
TAMEN · EXCIDIT · AUSIS

Here lies Phaethon, driver of Phoebus's chariot. Though he failed, he had at least ventured. Metrically my rendering was a disaster. And I had omitted that my (his!) body had been buried by water nymphs—why, goodness knows.

When the bell rang, the pupils left immediately, more quickly than usual. Maria Zeinstra came up to my desk and asked: "Do you always get so worked up?"

"Sorry," I said.

"No. I thought it was great. And it's a fantastic story. I didn't know it. Was that the end, or does it go on?"

And I told her about Phaethon's sisters, the Heliads, who changed into trees out of grief over their brother's death. "The way your rat changed into larvae, and then beetles."

"A roundabout way. But it isn't the same."

I wanted to tell her how magnificently Ovid describes the transformation into trees, how the mother, seeking to embrace her daughters for the last time, breaks away the bark and twigs framing their receding features, and how drops of blood ooze from the branches. Women, trees, blood, amber. But it was complicated enough as it was.

"All those changes of mine are metaphors for yours."

"Mine?"

"Well, in nature, I mean. Only, without the gods. There's no one to do it for us; we do it ourselves."

"Do what?"

"Change."

"Once we're dead, yes, but then we get the help of sexton beetles."

"It must be an enormous job to roll us up. That would make a pretty big carrion pellet. Pink." I could picture the scene. My small hands folded inward, my thinker's head poked into my belly.

She laughed. "We have other personnel for that. Maggots, worms. Very refined, too." She paused. Suddenly she looked about fourteen. "Do you believe in an afterlife?"

"No," I replied, truthfully. I am not even sure we

exist at all, I wanted to say, and then I went and said it.

"Oh, come off it." It sounded very North Hollandish. But suddenly she grabbed me by the lapels.

"Let's go for a drink." And in the same breath, stabbing her finger against my chest: "And what about this then? Doesn't this exist either?"

"This is my body," I said. It sounded pedantic.

"Yes, so Jesus Christ said, too. You do concede that it exists."

"Oh, yes."

"So what do you call it? 'Me,' 'I,' something like that?"

"Is your 'I' the same as ten years ago? Or the same as fifty years from now?"

"I hope I will be gone by then. But tell me exactly what *you* think we are, then."

"A cluster of composite, endlessly altering circumstances and functions which we address as 'I.' What else can I say? We act as if it is fixed and unchangeable, but it changes all the time, until it is discarded. But we keep on referring to it as 'I.' It's a sort of profession of the body."

"Wow."

"No, I mean it. This more or less random body or this collection of functions is required to be me during its lifetime. That sounds rather like some kind of job. Or doesn't it? Don't you agree?"

"You're slightly mad, if you ask me," she said. "But you tell a good story. And now I want a drink."

All right, she thought I was a funny little geezer, but my charred Phaethon had impressed her, I was very obviously available, and she was out for revenge. What makes Greek tragedies great is that this brand of psychological nonsense doesn't enter into them at all. I had wanted to tell her that, too, but unfortunately conversations consist for the most part of things one does not say. We are descendants, we do not have mythical lives, but psychological ones. And we know everything, we are always our own chorus.

"What I hate most about the whole affair," she said, "is that it's such a cliché." She was referring to Herfst and d'India, of course, and I wasn't quite sure yet whether she was right. The worst of it was, of course, d'India's mysteriousness. All the rest— young, pretty, pupil and teacher—that was the cliché. The mystery lay in the power the pupil had acquired.

"Do you see what I mean?"

Yes, I could see very well. What I could not see, but I didn't say so, was why d'India had chosen, of all people, this royal ass. But Plato had already coined a magic formula for that: "Love is in the one who loves, not in the one who is loved." It would be part of her life forever, it was a mistake, but she was entitled to that. It was all right for me; I had come close to something that resembled love for the first time in my life. Maria Zeinstra, being one of the free, took her freedom for granted; she cut straight through everything. It was as if this was the first time I had anything to do with the Dutch, or indeed with the *hoi polloi.* But one can't say such things.

She stood in a frozen dance posture between my four walls with my four thousand books and said: "I'm not illiterate myself, but this is going too far. D'you live here alone?"

"With Bat," I said. Bat was my cat. "I don't expect you'll even see him, because he's very shy." Five minutes later she was lying on the divan with Bat sprawled on top of her, the last rays of sunlight setting her red hair alight, two languid bodies, purring and murmuring, and I stood there as if I were the extension of my bookcases, waiting to be admitted into their intimacy. Bookish, somewhat ethereal women had been my domain until now, from timid to bitter, and all of them had been very good at explaining what was wrong with me. "Damn know-all," or "If you ask me, you don't even notice whether I'm here or not," were often-heard complaints, along with "Must you read *all* the time?" and "Do you ever think of anyone else?" Well, I did, as it happens, but on such occasions it was usually not of them. Besides, I simply had to get back to my books right away, because the company of most people, once the predictable events have taken their course, does not inspire conversation on my part. Indeed, I had grown skilled at getting rid of people, so that my circle was eventually limited to humans of the female sex who had the same idea as I. Tea, sympathy, urges, and subsequently the turning pages of a book. Growling red-haired women who knew all about sexton beetles and egg chambers were different, especially if they were curled on the divan with my cat in an undulating sequence of bellies, breasts, outstretched arms, laughing green eyes, if they pulled me toward them, took off my glasses, removed their clothes (to judge by the changing colors in my blurred vision) and said all sorts of things that I could not quite make out. Perhaps I even said the things people say in such circumstances. All I know is that everything was changing all the time, and that this had to be something like happiness.

When it was over, I felt as if I had swum the Channel. I retrieved my glasses and saw her leave with a wave. Bat looked at me as if he was about to gain the power of speech. I drank half a bottle of calvados and played the *"Ritorno d'Ulisse in patria"* until the neighbors started to bang the walls. Memory of lust is the most elusive of all, once lust becomes just an idea it becomes its own contradiction: absent, gone, and hence unthinkable. I know that I suddenly saw myself that evening, a man alone in a cube, surrounded by invisible others in adjacent cubes, and with tens of thousands of pages around me filled with descriptions of the same, but ever distinct, emotions of real or invented personages. I was moved by myself.

I would never write such a page, but the emotion I had felt during those past hours was mine forever. She had shown me a garden that had been closed to me. I was still shut out, but at least I had caught a glimpse of it. Glimpse is the wrong word. I had heard it. She had made a sound that did not belong to the world, that I had never heard before. It was the sound of a child, and at the same time of a pain no words can describe. Where that sound came from it must be impossible to live.

Evening in my memory, evening in Lisbon. The lamps in the city had been lit, my eyes were like a bird flying above the streets. It had grown cool, up there; the voices of the children had gone from the gardens; I saw the dark shadows of lovers, statues locked in embrace, lazily moving double-people. *Ignis mutat res,** I muttered, but *my* matter was not to be changed by any fire. I had already changed. Around me there was burning and melting, other two-headed creatures came to life, but I had long since lost my other, so red-haired, head, the female half of me had broken off. I had become a sort of cinder, a residue. My reason for being here, on this perhaps or perhaps not sought-after journey, could

* Fire changes matter.

well be a pilgrimage back to those days, and if so, I, like a medieval pilgrim, would have to visit all the sites of my brief holy life, all the stations where the past had a face. Like the lights in the city below I would descend to the river, the broad, secret stream of darkness, above which dancing lights traced their course, fluorescent letters on a blackboard. She had kept wanting to take those little ferries, an orgy of arrival and departure. Again and again we would see the city fade into the distance, then again the hills and docks on the other side, and so we seemed to belong only to the water, two light-headed fools among the workers, fools who were not part of the real world, but of the sun stabbing the water, the wind tugging at her dress. It had been her idea; she had invited me. We were not planning to travel together; she was going to Coimbra for a biology conference, after which she would spend a few days in Lisbon. I would join her there.

"And your husband?"

"Basketball tournament."

Revenge was known to me, from Aeschylus, but of basketball I knew nothing. For the sake of having her with me I had to tolerate the shadow of a tracksuited poet, but one who has taken the guise of a man in love will indiscriminately eat and drink platefuls of thistles, barrels of vinegar. The first evening I took her to Tavares in the Rua da Misericordia. A thousand mirrors in a cabinet encrusted with gold. It is not out of masochism that I will go there again tonight. I will go for the sake of verification. I want to see myself, and, sure enough, there I am, reflected in a forest of mirrors casting my shoulders farther and farther away, the lights of chandeliers sparkling in my thousand bespectacled eyes. A dense crowd of waiters hovers around me as I am led to my table, dozens of hands light dozens of candles, I receive a dozen menus and fifteen glasses of Sercial, and when they finally leave me alone I observe myself in multiplied form, my detestable back, my treacherous profile, my countless arms reaching to my one glass, my countless glasses of wine. But she is absent. Mirrors are useless; they retain nothing, not the living and not the dead; they are mercenary perjurers, nauseating in their glassy deference.

She had been excited by the decor, then. She had kept tilting her head, adjusting her angle of vision, appraising her body the way only women can, seeing it as others saw it. All those red-haired women would sleep with me that night, even those farthest away, the splashes of red in the black field of bobbing waiters, and I, I was shrinking, and when she laid her hand on mine and all those tender hands fluttered across the image, her look excluded me. My stature diminished while hers increased. She soaked up the stares of guests and waiters. She never existed as vividly as then. The mirrors had been so crowded with her reflections that I still expect to see her in them now, but she is not there. Somewhere in the archival software behind that gleaming forehead of the man observing me, that's where she is, talking, laughing, eating, flirting with the waiters, a woman with white, flashing teeth biting into the port as if it were meat. I know that woman; she isn't yet the stranger she would become later. That evening we had walked. Even after twenty years I needed no bread crumbs to retrace the route we had taken. I follow the trajectory of my desire. I was drawn to that strange structure on the Praça do Comercio, where two columns rise from the gently rippling water like a gateway to the ocean and the world beyond. The dictator's name is carved in the marble, but he has gone now, taking his anachronistic empire with him, leaving the water to pursue its slow erosion of those columns. Can you keep track of my tenses? They are all past tenses, my thoughts were wandering; do excuse me. Here I am, back again, the imperfect reflecting on the past, simple past versus pluperfect. My present tense was a slip; it applied only to now, to you, although you are nameless. After all, we are both present here, still.

I sat down where I had sat with her and invoked her memory, but she held back. All I had was a fan of impotent words straining to denote the color of her hair once more, vermilion vying with auburn, crimson, blood-red, brass, rust, chestnut, and not one of those colors was hers; her red eluded me as soon as I was parted from her, and yet I continued to search for something that could register at least her appearance, as if it were necessary here, in this place of farewell, to draw up a protocol, as if it were work, *officium*. But try as I might, the seat beside me remained empty, just as empty as the chair in front of the Café A Brasileira by the statue of Pessoa in the Rua Garrett. His solitude at least had been self-imposed. If anyone had been sitting beside him, it would have been himself, one of his three alter egos come to join him in drinking himself silently and deliberately to death in the dark shadows beyond, among the high-backed chairs with brass-studded black leather upholstery, the distorting mirrors of the heteronyms, the Greek temples floating across the walls, and the massive clock (by A. Romero), all the way in the back of the narrow space, drinking its fill of time just like the customers sipping the sweet black liquid of death from small white cups.

I tried to remember what we had talked about that evening. If my memory serves me, we had talked about nothing. We had sat there in silence, surrounded by the same people who were there now, the dozing lottery-ticket seller, the sailors talking in low voices at the water's edge, the solitary figure of a man with his oh-so-soft radio, girls exchanging secrets. No, this particular night would not bring back the words; they were drifting around somewhere, they had been stolen for other mouths, other sentences, they had been absorbed into lies, newspaper reports, letters, or they were lying on some beach or other on the far side of the world, washed up by the tide, meaningless, unintelligible.

I got up, ran my fingers over the worn inscription on the column that spoke of the empire that would last forever. I saw the water ebbing away in the dark, leaving behind the city like an empty carcass, a shell into which I would crawl as if my bed were not in some other city, on the shores of another, more northern, sea. The night porter greeted me as if he had seen me yesterday and the day before, and handed me the key to my room before I could ask. I did not switch on the light and felt my way around like someone suddenly struck blind. I had no desire to see myself in the mirror, and I did not feel like reading. I'd had a surfeit of words. How long I slept I do not know, but again it seemed that an unspeakable force was tugging at me, that I was borne along by a current against which a poor swimmer such as myself was powerless, that an enormous, all-encompassing wave slapped me down on a deserted beach. There I lay, very still, water dripping from my face, and through those tears I saw myself lying in bed in Amsterdam. I slept, tossing and turning my head, and crying, still clutching the photograph from the evening newspaper in my left hand. I looked at the little Japanese alarm clock I always keep next to my bed. What sort of time can this be in which time stands still? It wasn't any later than it had been when I went to sleep. The dark shape at my feet had to be Night Owl, successor to Bat. I could see that the man in Amsterdam wanted to wake up, he was thrashing about, his right hand groping for his glasses, but it was not he who switched on the light; it was me, here in Lisbon.

# Two

This is, I believe, *it:* not the crude anguish of
physical death but the incomparable pangs of the
mysterious mental maneuver needed to pass
from one state of being to another.
Easy, you know, does it, son.

—VLADIMIR NABOKOV,
*Transparent Things*

Anyone who is used to keeping a class of thirty pupils under control has learned to be quick-sighted. A boy, two old men, two men of my own age. The woman standing somewhat aloof like a figurehead was harder to place, perhaps that first impression was the best: a figurehead. She beckoned the dinghy that was to take us to the ship lying at anchor in midstream. It was still early. There was a pale mist; the ship was a blurred, dark mass. What struck me most was the intensity of the boy's expression, eyes like gun barrels. I recognized the kind; you see them on the *meseta,* the high Spanish plain. The kind that can see far into the distance in the white light of the sun. There was no conversation as yet. We knew at once that we belonged together. My dreams have always borne a disturbing resemblance to life, as if even in my sleep I could not come up with something new, but now it was the other way around, now at last my life resembled a dream. Dreams are closed systems, in which everything fits to perfection.

I looked at the absurd statue of Christ high on the south bank, arms outstretched, ready to jump. "Ready to jump," that was what she had said. Seeing the statue again I suddenly remembered what we had talked about, that evening beside the water. She had wanted to explain all sorts of things about the brain, cells, impulses, cerebellum, cortex, the whole butcher's shop which reputedly monitors and controls everything we do, and I had told her that I loathed phrases like "gray matter," that cells reminded me of prisons, and that I had often fed Bat one of those little blood-veined puddings. In short, I had made it clear that it was by no means essential for my thought process to know precisely which recesses of that spongy organ were being set to work. She had retorted that I was worse than medieval man, that Vesalius's lancet had already liberated the spiritually indigent like me from the prison of their bodies, to which I had of course said that all her razor-sharp blades and laser beams had never been able to fathom the hidden kingdom of memory, and that to me Mnemosyne was infinitely more real than the notion that all my memories, including those which I would eventually have of her, were stashed in a piggy bank made of a gray, beige or cream-colored, lobed and altogether rather slimy substance, and then she had kissed me and I had muttered something to those urgent, searching, yearning lips, but she had simply silenced my babbling mouth with hers, and we had sat there until dawn's rosy fingers touched the Christ figure on the far side of the river.

The old ferryman taking us across started the engine; the city dipped out of sight behind us. Once we were on the ship we remained close together; we were shown our cabins, and a few minutes later we were all back on deck, each having chosen his position at the rail, a bizarre pleiad, in which constellation the boy became the most distant star because he had positioned himself at the furthermost point of the stern, as if his narrow shoulders denoted the vanishing point of the earth. When he turned, I could see who he was; he had the profile of Icarus in the relief in the Villa Albani in Rome, the body hardly more than a child's, the somewhat overlarge head, the right hand resting on the fateful wing just fashioned by his father. And as if he could read my thoughts, the boy now touched the flagstaff without flag pointing at the departing world. For that was how it was. We were standing still, and the Belém Tower, the hills of the city, the wide estuary, the tiny island with the lighthouse were all being sucked toward a single focus. Time was making the visible world shrink so that it becomes a line on the horizon that lets itself be stretched more and more slowly, till the world is just a vaporous thing. This infinite slowness was, of course, swiftness, as you know better than anyone else because you must live in this dream-time forever, in which contraction and expansion cancel each other out at will.

The last smudge of land had disappeared from the horizon, and still we stood there motionless, only the foam in the wake of the ship and the first vacillations of the great rolling dance belied our immobility. The water of the ocean looked black; it reeled, tossed, sailed away into itself, furling and unfurling, glistening sheets of liquid metal collapsing soundlessly, merging, each wave plowing a furrow for the next to fold into, the inexorable, perpetual change into perpetually the same.

All of us stared at the process, all those different eyes, which would become so familiar to me during the next few days, seemed to be mesmerized by the water. Days! Now that I say the word out loud I can hear how insubstantial it sounds. If you were to ask me what is the worst predicament of all, I would say the dearth of measure. We are totally dependent on it. Life is too empty for our taste, too open-ended; we have invented all sorts of things to cling to: names, dates, measurements, anecdotes. So just let me be. I have nothing more than my conventions and so I will go on referring quite simply to day and hour, even though our voyage seemed to take not the least notice of their dictates. The Sioux did not have a word for time, but I haven't reached that point yet, although I am a fast learner. Sometimes there was just the unending night, and then the days would flit by like nervous moments across the horizon, pausing only long enough to paint the ocean twice over in all shades of red and then to restore it to the dark.

The first hours no one spoke. A priest, an airline pilot, a child, a teacher, a journalist, an academic. They made up the group, someone or no one had decided: these were to be the mirrors in which we would see ourselves. You knew where we were going, and it was enough to know you knew. But I can't talk to you like this: you can't be both in the story and not in it. And I am not almighty, so I don't know what was going on in the hidden thoughts of the others. As far as I was concerned, there was an atmosphere of peace that I at any rate had never experienced. They all seemed to have some preoccupation, to be meditating on a private thought or memory; sometimes they would disappear below for a spell, or you would see someone in the distance conversing with one of the crew or walking to and fro near the bridge. The boy was often to be seen on the foredeck; no one bothered him there. The priest would be reading in a corner of the lounge; the academic kept to his cabin for much of the time; the pilot peered through his telescope next to the deckhouse at night; the journalist played poker with the barman and drank; and I looked out over those eternally swaying canvases, pondered, and translated the malicious odes in Book II. Yes, Horace—who else? The undoing of Rome, the lechery, the dissolution, the profligacy. *Quid non imminuit dies?* What is not destroyed by time? "Why do you translate 'dies' as 'time'?" Lisa d'India had asked.

Even now, on this trip, her question made me smile. Her days were over, she had run out of time so long ago, and yet we had once stood face to face at my desk, she with James Michie's verse translation in the Penguin Classics edition, I with my own scribbled lines, and even now I can still hear her voice, the burin of those five Latin words, *damnosa quid non imminuit dies,* followed by the northern rendering, which has to use nine words to say the selfsame thing: *Time corrupts all. What has it not made worse?* I had wanted to make some clever remark about the singularity of the single day, which permits interpretation as a plethora of time where all days are stored, and I had got entangled in all manner of nonsense about our calendar being the abacus of the uncountable, and suddenly I had seen the disappointment in her eyes, the moment when it dawns on the pupil that the teacher is skirting the issue, not knowing the answer. I continued to waffle for a while about hour and duration, but I had already betrayed my ineptitude. When she walked away like a woman, I knew that I had disappointed a child, and that too is part and parcel of my profession, the corruption of minors. Faced with the erosion of your own authority, you relegate them to a world without answers. It is not pleasant to impose adulthood on anyone, especially if they are still glowing with youth. But I gave up teaching so long ago.

The priest strolled along by the rail. He was already, so it seemed, almost weightless; the motion of the ship was making him levitate. He had introduced himself as "Dom Antonio Fermi," and when I had signaled brief surprise, he had explained the Dom as: "*Dominus,* of the Benedictine Order." Fermi, Harris, Deng, Mussert, Carnero, Dekobra—those words were our names. We had proffered each other portions of our lives, and now we were sailing over the ocean with all those unfamiliar, as yet undigested fragments. They could have been other people's lives, other forms of coincidence. If one isn't traveling alone, one is surrounded by strangers. "I saw you talking to yourself," he said.

Once again, but out loud this time, I recited the last verse of the sixth ode. I could not deny myself this luxury. It's not every day that I encounter someone to whom Latin is still a living language. He fell in by the second line, in his reedy, old man's voice—two Roman herons at sea.

"I didn't realize that the Benedictines knew Horace by heart."

He laughed. "Not many of them do. But one has always been something else before becoming a follower of Saint Benedict," and he danced off again. I knew a little more about him now, but what was

I to do with all this information? Wasn't this a journey that I was supposed to be making by myself? What did I have in common with them, or they with me? "I had a thousand lives and I took only one," I had read somewhere once. Did that mean, in my case, that I could have had these lives, too? I had, of course, not elected to be born in twentieth-century Holland, any more than Professor Deng had chosen to be Chinese. The odds in favor of Father Fermi's being born a Catholic were of course higher in Italy than elsewhere, but Italy itself, or the twentieth century instead of the third or the fifty-third, details of that nature were of course subject to the laws of chance. Infuriating. To a large extent, you already existed before you had anything to do with it at all.

Alonso Carnero couldn't help it that his grandmother had been shot by the Fascists in the Spanish Civil War, and we could go on in the same vein, holding up the mirrors of our exemplary contingency for each other to behold. If I had been obliged to say "I" to the persona of Peter Harris, I would have been not only a drunk and a womanizer, but also an expert on Third World debt, and if I had been Flight Captain Dekobra not only would I have had the ramrod physique and piercing ice-blue eyes I had always craved, but also I would have traversed the ocean many times in my DC-8, the same ocean I was now dawdling over in the iron hull of this nameless ship. If I were to engross myself in the depths of their lives I would need a life as long as theirs, and since that was impossible I had to make do with irrelevant fragments, *faits divers*. Professor Deng had obtained a Ph.D. in the distant past with a thesis comparing early occidental and Chinese astronomy. Great. Harris was not partial to blondes, so he lived in Bangkok. Good for him. He traveled the Third World as a journalist—"Their debt, my gain." Quite so. And Father Fermi had once upon a time been a parish priest at the Duomo in Milan. "Do you know the cathedral?"

I did indeed. I would have liked to present him with a copy of Dr. Strabo's insipid *Guide to Northern Italy,* in which I had managed to reduce that lyrical stone mastodon to a species of Woolworth's for herds of tourists.

"For me that building stood on a par with hell." Quite a statement for a priest. "For years I was father-confessor there. At least you never had to do that." Right he was. I tried to imagine it, but couldn't.

"As soon as I stepped out of the sacristy into the Duomo I would feel sick. I felt like a floor cloth, waiting for them to wipe off their lives on me. You have no idea to what lengths people will go. You have never seen their faces at such close quarters either, the hypocrisy, the lewdness, their sordid beds, their greed. And they kept coming back, and one kept being forced to forgive them. But in some horrible way that made one an accomplice, one was drawn into the liaisons they were unable to break off, into the sordidness of their characters. I fled from all that, and went into a monastery. I could no longer bear the human voice unless it was singing." And once more he had danced off.

My place at the ship's rail was *my* confessional. I had discovered that if you took up the same position day after day, the others would come to you of their own accord. Only Alonso Carnero never came. He had his own post. Once, I went over to him. The woman had been standing beside him, and together they looked into the black hole of night. There were no stars, and for the first time in my life I experienced the physical sensation of the underworld. As the voyage proceeded, everything I had ever read out in class as fiction became more and more real. The ocean, like Phaethon's fatal ride, had been one of my hit numbers, and I could even impersonate the sea, how it lay black and malevolent, stirring around the flat earth, the terrifying element in which familiar objects lost their contours, the amorphous residue of the primordial substance from which everything had originated, the chaotic, dangerous obverse of the world, that which our forebears had called the Sin of Nature, the ever-present threat of a new Flood. And beyond, in the West, where the sun sank and the light stole away, abandoning men to the devices of that other shapeless element, the night, was the ocean in which Atlas once stood and which bore his name, and behind that the dark domain of death called Tartarus, Saturn's place of banishment, *Saturno tenebrosa in Tartara misso**— how can I ever explain the thrill of pronouncing the Latin words? It has something to do with physical enjoyment, a reversed form of eating. What a deranged Socrates this teacher had been, he who had taken his pupils to the seaside one day—the few who had not fallen over laughing, that is. A storm was blowing as the little train took us from IJmuiden to the underworld, but once at the far end of the pier it was real enough, the thundering sea pounding the basalt blocks as if it wanted to devour them, the sky heavy with ominous clouds, the rain lashing our solitary group—only five of us—and between the screams of the gulls I worked overtime, shouting westward to make myself heard over the storm, and of course there behind that seething mass of water lay the secret world of shadows with its four deathly rivers. With every word I shouted the gulls screeched their echoes of Orpheus and the Styx like furies, and I remember the white, transparent face of my dearest pupil because it is in such faces that myths come true. I stood there like a demented gnome face to face with the generation of camouflaged death, ranting on about eternal mists and destruction. Socrates in IJmuiden. The next day d'India had given me a poem, something to do with stormy weather and feeling lonely. I had folded it

* Saturn, who was sent to the dark Tartarus.

73

up and put it in my pocket; it had no *form,* it resembled the modern poetry you read in magazines, and because I didn't want to tell her that, I had said nothing, and now, here, on board this ship, I wondered what had become of the poem. Somewhere among my papers, somewhere in a room in Amsterdam.

He had her eyes, the boy. Latin eyes. He watched me approaching him, did not look away. When I was close, the woman lifted her hand from his shoulder and vanished, as if she had evaporated.

"Our guide," Captain Dekobra had called her, at one point, with a mixture of mockery and respect. She was there and yet she wasn't, but, present or absent, it was she who had kept our motley group together, without anyone seeming to wonder why. Once I was at Alonso Carnero's side I had forgotten what I wanted to say. All I could come up with was: "What are you thinking about?" He shrugged and said: "About the fish in the sea." And naturally that made me think of them too, of all those unseen, unresponsive life-forms in the thousands of meters beneath us. I shuddered, and went to my cabin.

That night I dreamed again that I was in my room in Amsterdam. Did I do nothing but sleep? I wanted to rouse myself and found that I was switching on the light in my cabin, confused, sweaty. I never wanted to see that sleeping figure again, that open mouth and the blind eyes, the desolation of that heaving, restless body. Since Maria Zeinstra, I had not spent another night with a woman. It was, I had thought at the time, my last chance of experiencing real life, whatever that might mean. A sense of belonging—together, to the world, that sort of thing. Once, I had even mentioned children. Derision. "We're not letting crazy ideas enter our bald little head, are we?" she had said, as if addressing an entire classroom. "You and children! Some people ought never to have children, and you are one of them."

"You talk as if I had a terrible disease. If you think I'm such a creep, why do you go to bed with me?"

"Because I'm very good at keeping things apart. And because I feel like it, if you want to know."

"Then I suppose you'll have to have your babies with your basketball poet."

"Who I have them with is my business. But it won't be with a schizoid garden gnome from the antique shop. And you are the last person who ought to be discussing Arend Herfst."

Arend Herfst. Third person. The myoma with its built-in poetic grin.

"Besides, why don't you try writing a poem yourself sometime. And some exercise wouldn't do you any harm." That was true; then perhaps I would have been able to fly instead of sail. To flee that cabin, stretch my arms out wide and fly away, the

75

sleeping ship under my feet, the lonely watchman in the yellow light, our ferryman, detaching myself from all those others, into the deeper darkness.

I got dressed and went up on deck. They were all there; it was like a conspiracy. They were standing around Captain Dekobra, scanning the sky with the telescope. It could never have been the same night, for there are nights when the stars are out to strike fear into us, and this was one of them. I had never seen so many stars. I felt as if I could hear them above the sound of the sea, calling to us, longing, angry, jeering. Due to the absence of all other light, they encircled us like a dome, light-holes, light-gravel, laughing at the names and numbers we had given them long ago in that belated second of our appearance on earth. They were ignorant of their names, of the bizarre shapes our limited eyes had once seen in them—scorpions, horses, serpents, lions of burning gas—and far below them we stood, suffused with the ineradicable notion that we were standing at the very center, with far beneath us another closed dome, a safe, spherical screen all around us which would present itself forever in the same guise.

The sea glistened and rocked, I held on to the rail and looked at the others. There was nothing to prove it, but they had changed—no; they had changed *again*. Things were disappearing, lines were missing. I kept seeing part of someone's mouth or not, or an eye, for the tiniest fraction of a second their identity would be gone; then I would see the

76

body of one through that of another, as if their solidity were being dismantled, and at the same time the radiance of what was still visible intensified. If it didn't sound so absurd, I would have said that they were luminous. I held my hands in front of my eyes and saw nothing but my hands. Miracles never happen to me, so there was no reason whatsoever for the others to give me such strange looks as I approached.

"See the Hunter?" Captain Dekobra asked Alonso Carnero. "That's Orion." The celestial giant's body inclined forward. "He's hunting, stalking his prey. But he's wary, because he's blind. Do you see that clear, brilliant star at his feet, in front of him? That is Sirius, that's his dog. Take a look through this and you can see him breathe."

The boy raised the heavy telescope and gazed through it for a long while, in silence.

"Now you go up a little, along his belt, Alnilam, Alnitak, Mintaka"—he intoned the words as if they were a mantra— "then you continue up to his right shoulder, *ibt al jakrah,* the armpit, that's Betelgeuse, four hundred times the size of the sun . . ."

Alonso Carnero lowered the telescope and turned to Dekobra. There it was again: the dark eyes staring at the ice-blue ones, two forms of looking which bored through each other, not faces anymore, just eyes. A fraction of a second, and then their faces flowed back into shape in the night air. The others did not see this, or said nothing. But I did not speak either. Four hundred times the size of the

77

sun—Maria Zeinstra had told me that too; I had already lost my virginity. She knew everything I did not want to know. As it was, I was not familiar with the night sky due to the thick glasses through which I peered at the world anyway, but I could still distinguish the Hunter, I knew how he climbed onto the still-slumbering world as the night grew old; for me he was the exile from the ninth book of the *Odyssey,* the lover of rosy-fingered Dawn. I did not want to know how hot or how old his stars were, nor how far away he was.

"You'll just have to remain ignorant, then."

I can hear her voice next to me, but she is not there.

"What's the point of knowing the world as you know it?" I had asked. "All those silly figures shattering us with their zeros!"

Amazement. Head held aslant. Red hair hanging like a banner to one side. Orion has almost dissolved into the light of day. We haven't slept yet.

"How do you mean?"

"Cells, enzymes, light-years, hormones. Behind everything I see, you always see something else."

"Because it's there."

"And so?"

"I don't want to spend what little time I have here on earth groping around like a blind man."

She got up. "And now I must go home to await the great hunter. I thought Sicilians took better care of their children."

"She's not a child."

"No." It sounded bitter. "They've all seen to that all right."

Silence. "I must go," she said. "His lordship is jealous, too."

Whether I might be jealous she did not ask.

"Castor and Pollux," I heard Captain Dekobra say. Truly, it seemed as if everyone wanted me to return to my past. The blackboard of the sky was inscribed in Latin, but I was no longer a teacher. "Orion, Taurus. Then up again to Perseus, Auriga . . ." I followed the pointing finger tracing the different configurations, which now, like us, seemed to be swaying gently. At some point, said the captain, those configurations would be pulled apart, unraveled, redistributed over a future sky. What had bound them together was the accident of our vision during the past few thousand years, that which we had wished to see in them. They were no more united than a crowd of passersby on the Champs-Elysées; those heavenly figures were simply brief moments in the history of time—although the moments were rather protracted by our standards. Thousands of years from now the Great Bear would have vanished, Sagittarius would have stopped shooting his arrows, their constituent stars would have pursued their own course, their slow movement in relation to one another would efface the signs as we knew them: Boötes would have stopped guarding the Bear, Perseus would never again rescue

Andromeda from her rock, Andromeda would no longer recognize her mother Cassiopeia. Of course there would be new, equally fortuitous constellations (yes, Captain, I do know *stella* means star), but who will be there to name them? The mythology that had dominated my life would have been obliterated by then, indeed, it already had been; it owed its very survival in the world to those constellations. Names arise only when there is something living to denote. It was the sheer presence of the configuration that made people think of Perseus, so that they still knew, as Captain Dekobra did, that it was the head of the Gorgon Medusa that he held aloft, and that it was her evil eye that blinked at us, malevolent, defiant, in a final flash of danger.

"The Pool of the gods," said Professor Deng.

We all turned to him. He pointed toward Auriga, the Charioteer. A chariot, a pool. He spoke very softly; his face seemed to be alight. I was struck by his resemblance to Father Fermi. They had to be equally old, but "old" was no longer a category to which their lives could be assigned. They had overcome time, they were transparent, released, they were far ahead of us.

> *"I took my dragons to water in the Pool*
> *of Heaven,*
> *and tethered them to the Fusang tree.*
> *I broke a branch off the Ruo-tree to beat*
> *the sun . . .*

"You see," he said, "we gave the stars names, too, but they were not the same names as yours. It was so early in history we were not yet acquainted with your mythology." His eyes flickered with irony. "Time was too short; it would have been too short even if it had been thousands of years. . . . My whole life has been devoted to this subject."

"And the poem?" I asked. "We had horses charging across the sky, not dragons."

"It is by Qu Yuan," said Professor Deng, "but you probably don't know him. One of our classics. Earlier than your Ovid."

He sounded apologetic. "Qu Yuan was also banished. He, too, censured his lord for gathering base characters around him, for the corruption of the royal court." He laughed. "Our sun, too, was driven across the sky, but the charioteer was not a man, like your Phoebus Apollo, but a woman. And we didn't have one sun, but ten. They slept in the branches of the Fusang tree, an enormous tree at the westernmost tip of the earth, where your Atlas stands. Our poets and shamans treated the constellations as if they really existed. Your Auriga is our Pool of Heaven, a real, existing lake in which the deity washes his hair. There is also a song in which the Sun God drinks wine with the Great Bear."

We looked at the spot in the heavens which had now been transformed into a pool, and I wanted to say that Orion had always struck me as a very real hunter, but suddenly everyone had something to say. Father Fermi started on about the pilgrims' road to Santiago de Compostela being known as the Milky Way in the Middle Ages. He had been on that pilgrimage himself, on foot, and because the only Milky Way we could see at that moment was the veil of light floating overhead, that was where we saw him now, taking his light-footed dance steps. Captain Dekobra explained how he had learned to navigate by the stars, and then we saw him, too, flying way above us in his lonely aureole, the hum of engines reverberating in his cocoon of cold silence, the panels with trembling dials, and above him, nearer still to him than to us now, the same, or other, beacons on which Chinese and Greeks, Babylonians and Egyptians had hung their names unaware that beyond those myriad stars there were, hidden away, as many more unseen bodies as there were grains of sand on all the beaches in the world, and that no mythology would ever have enough gods and heroes to name them.

Harris, who had until now listened in silence, said that the only times he had looked up at the stars from a supine position were when, not for the first time, he had been thrown drunk out of some bar, and when we laughed, Alonso Carnero told us how, in that invisible village on the *meseta* that was his home, while everyone was watching television in the evening, he would shoot his catapult at the Great Bear—and now we could see him, too—and how he had imagined that his pebble might actually travel the entire distance and hit the beast in its flank. We had all wanted something from those coolly sparkling points of light—something they would never give us.

"It's getting light," said Captain Dekobra.

"Or whatever," said Harris.

We laughed, and I saw that Professor Deng saw in my face, or, rather, did not see, what I had seen earlier in his.

"Am I still here?" I asked.

"Oh, yes, you are," he said, and because he was standing precisely in the path of the rising sun a nimbus of gold appeared around his head, so it seemed that his face had now truly vanished, and perhaps it had. It was not until I took a step to one side that I saw him again.

" 'I left early in the morning from the ford in the Heavenly Pool, and at night I arrived at the western reaches of the world . . .' " Professor Deng declaimed, and when I looked at him questioningly: "Qu Yuan again. For our spirits—and for yours too, I presume?—time passes much more quickly than ordinary time. He is a great poet; in a future life you should really study him. The opening lines of his epic poem tell of his divine ancestry, at the close he announces his intention to quit this corrupt world to seek the company of the holy dead."

"I'm not sure where the ford in the heavens is," said Dekobra, "but it happened pretty often that I would be in the far West at night, even though only that morning I had got up in the East."

"If you don't know where you're going, speed doesn't make much difference," muttered Harris.

No one answered, as if he had broken a taboo. He shrugged and took a swig from a silver flask he carried in his pocket.

"I can't stand daylight anymore," he said, and disappeared. I went to the stern of the ship. The divided furrow behind us stretched away to the horizon. I liked standing at the exact midpoint, the iron arc of the rail holding me in a fond embrace. The wake was the color of gold and blood.

"I can't stand daylight anymore." I knew that if I turned now I would see the others as a broken pleiad, only because I had stepped out of the formation. But I had to stand there, alone, and think. Those were the words she had spoken at the end of the last-but-one day of my teaching career, or at the beginning of the last day, if you like. Those two days had not been bridged by sleep; perhaps that was why it seemed to be the longest day in my life. Let us agree that I was happy that day, all right? In my case, that sort of emotion is always coupled with a sense of loss, and hence with melancholy, but the undercurrent had been happiness. She never wanted to say she loved me ("Go and ask your mother that kind of thing"), but was infinitely cunning at picking times, codes, places for rendezvous. In any case, I could actually still bear the sight of myself in those days, and a hint of this must have been noticeable to others ("For someone so ugly you're actually quite good-looking"). Anyway, since everything has to rhyme in my life, I devoted the last lesson I would ever give to Plato's *Phaedo*.

I may be a rotten travel-guide writer, but I was a talented teacher. I was able to lead my pupils like docile sheep past the thorny hedges of syntax and grammar. I could make the sun-chariot's collision with the earth so lurid as to set the entire classroom on fire, and I could, as I did that day, make Socrates die with a dignity that they would never forget as long (or as short) as they lived. First some sheepish sniggers about my nickname ("No, ladies and gentle-men, I have no intention of bestowing that favor upon you today") and thereafter silence. For it wasn't true what I had said. I was actually about to die there. "Whenever colleague Mussert has done his Socrates act, the kids are as quiet as mice for the rest of the day," Arend Herfst had observed, and for once he was right. The classroom had been transformed into an Athenian prison, my friends were gathered around me, at sunset I would drink from the cup of poison. I could have escaped this fate, I could have fled from Athens, but I had not done so. I would spend one last day with my friends who were my pupils, I would teach them how a man faces death, and I would not be alone in my dying, I would die in their company, as a man whose place is in the world. I, my other I, knew I had to guide my pupils past tenuous abstractions to the higher chemistry in which the man about to die seeks to divorce soul from body. He adduced proof upon proof of the immortality of the soul, but beneath all those ratiocinations yawned the chasm of death, the absence of the soul.

The ugly body sitting there, talking, at times patting the nape of a neck, walking about and thinking and emitting sounds, would presently die; it would be burned or buried, the others watching and listening to the sounds with which it consoled them, consoled itself. Of course they wanted to believe that the uncouth, rough-hewn form before them contained a royal, invisible, immortal substance which was no substance, something which, once that strange septuagenarian body finally lay supine, grotesquely inanimate, would be liberated at last from all that obstructs pure reason, free from desire, which would travel, depart the world, and yet remain or return—the impossible. That I myself did not believe these things was irrelevant, I acted the part of a believer. What *I* was thinking that afternoon wasn't the point. The point was that here was a man consoling his friends whereas he was the one who deserved consolation, and that it was possible for a man to devote the final hours of his life to intellectual exercise, not to the formulation of arguments per se, but to the volley of ideas, options, inklings, contradictions, to the arches spanning the distance from one mind to another in that confined space, to the astounding potential of the human intellect for self-reflection, for reversal of opinion, for weaving webs of questions and then securing them in the void where certainty can deny itself.

And again, as with Phaethon, I showed them the earth from above, my pupils who had seen the earth a hundred times on television, a blue-white ball suspended in space; they, who had always known that our gleaming balloon was not the center of the universe, had now become the pupils of that other Socrates; they flew with him away from that Athenian cell and perceived their so much more mysterious world "like a ball made of twelve pieces of leather," as the real Socrates had put it. A splendid, multicolored world set with gems, of which the place where they had to lead their daily lives and whence their old friend must soon depart was but a pale, miserable reflection. And I told them that within that same earth now seen from above, which is at once the real and yet not the real earth, numberless streams flow beneath the surface into the immense subterranean lagoon called Tartarus, water that had no bed or bottom, and I leapt to and fro in front of the class, my short arms conducting vast bodies of water through the room just as that other man, from whom I had borrowed the words, had made them flow through that prison cell from which he would never escape. I became a huge pumping station, dividing the waters over the earth. And I told them, he told them, of the four great rivers of the farthest Underworld, of Okeanos, the largest, which encircles the earth, of the Acheron threading its course through deathly desolation and discharging into a lake on whose banks the souls of the dead must wait for new lives, of regions of fire and mud and rocks, and always those human dreams of eternal recompense and eternal punishment, and I left those poor souls standing there in the half-light, waiting, I said, like a bunch of workmen at a bus stop on a foggy winter morning.

And then it is all over. I withdraw, I create a vast distance between myself and the front row. Now I am about to die. I gaze into the eyes of my pupils just as he must have gazed into the eyes of his. I know exactly who is Simmias and who Cebes, and all the time Lisa d'India had assuredly been Crito, who, at the bottom of his heart, does not believe in immortality. All I have said has been in vain. I stand still in the corner nearest to the blackboard and look at Crito, my dearest pupil. She is sitting pale-faced and upright at her desk. Then I tell them that a tragic poet would now say, "The voice of fate calls." I want to bathe myself, so that the women need not wash my body when I am gone. Then Crito asks if there is anything they can still do for me, for my children, and I reply that all I ask of my friends is that they take care of themselves, that is the main thing, and when Crito then asks how I wish to be buried, I tease him, saying that he'll have to get hold of me first, and by that of course I mean my soul, that volatile thing, and I reproach him for seeing me only as a prospective corpse, for not believing in my invisible journey, in my immortality, but only in what I leave behind, the body before him.

And then I go away to bathe myself, yet I am standing in the corner of the classroom, and Crito comes with me, yet remains seated at her desk, and I see how their eyes are focused on me and then I am back again, talking with the jailer, who has come to say that it is time to drink the poison. He knows, that man knows, that I shall not rant and rave like the other condemned men to whom he must offer the deadly cup, and then Crito insists that I eat something first and says the sun is still shining on the mountaintops, that it has not yet sunk, and then we all look up at the mountains on the playground and there it is, a red glow over blue mountains. But I refuse. I know there are others who wait till the very last moment, but I do not want to be one of them. "No, Crito," I say. "What would I gain by delaying the moment of taking poison, by clinging to life like an unwilling child?" And so Crito made a sign to the jailer with the cup, and I ask what I must do and he says: "Nothing; just drink it and walk around. Then your legs will become heavy and you will lie down. You need do nothing." And he hands me the cup, and I drink slowly, and as I return the empty nonexistent cup to the invisible jailer, I look into Crito's eyes, which are the eyes of d'India, and there I stop—we don't want a Grand Guignol show. I do not lie down on the floor, I do not let the jailer feel my legs to check whether there is still any sensation left, I stay where I am and die and read out the closing verses in which a great coldness creeps up on me and I say something about owing a cock to Aesculapius, which I say to show them that I want to die in this world, the world of reality. And then it is the end. The sheet is lifted from Socrates' face, the eyes in a fixed stare. Crito closes them, and the open mouth. But we don't do any of those things.

Now comes the delicate moment when they have to leave the classroom. They have no desire to talk, nor have I. I turn away and look for something in my briefcase. I know the effect Plato's theories of the body being a hindrance to the soul have had on Christianity, and I deplore it; and I also know that Socrates is part of the eternal misunderstanding of Western civilization, but his death never fails to move me, especially when I'm acting the part myself.

When I turn around, most of them have left. A few red eyes, the boys with those averted heads as if to say "Don't think I'm impressed." A lot of noise in the corridor, too loud laughter. But d'India stayed; she really was crying.

"Stop that immediately," I said. "You obviously haven't understood a word of what I've been saying."

"That's not why I'm crying." She was putting her books into her satchel.

"What's the matter then?" Stupid question number 807.

"Everything."

A divine image in tears. Not an uplifting sight.

" 'Everything' covers rather a lot of ground."

"I suppose it does." And then, vehemently, "You don't believe it yourself, about the immortality of the soul."

"No."

"Then why do you tell the story as if you did?"

"The situation in that cell has nothing to do with any ideas I might get into my head."

"But why don't you believe it?"

"Because he tries to prove it four times over. A sure sign of weakness, that is. I don't think he believed it himself, not really. But the point is not immortality."

"What is the point, then?"

"The point is that we are capable of thinking about immortality. That is what sets us apart."

"Without our believing in it, you mean?"

"If you ask me, yes. But I'm not very good at this sort of discussion."

She got up. She was taller than I, and I automatically took a step backward. Then suddenly she looked straight at me and said: "If I break it off with Arend Herfst, does that mean you'll lose Mrs. Zeinstra?"

Bull's-eye. I had only just died and here I was having to act a part in another play. Unthinkable that the real Socrates should ever have been drawn into a conversation of this nature. Every period in history has its own punishments, and ours has a multitude.

"Let's forget we ever had this conversation," I said, finally. She wanted to say something in return, but at that moment Maria Zeinstra burst into the classroom, and because she was going at her usual speed she was in the middle of the room by the time she noticed Lisa d'India. Such things happen in a split second: red hair bowling into the room, black hair storming out, a pupil holding a handkerchief to her mouth.

"A child, after all," said Maria Zeinstra with satisfaction.

"Not really."

"Don't tell me."

Then we noticed the book Lisa d'India had left behind. She picked it up and opened it.

"Plato. Well, you win. It was all blood vessels and arteries in my class today."

As she put the book down an envelope slipped out from between the pages. She looked at it and held it up to me.

"For you."

"For me?"

"If you're Herman Mussert, it's for you. May I read it?"

"I'd rather you didn't."

"Why not?"

"Because your name certainly isn't Herman Mussert."

She snorted with sudden anger. I reached out to take the letter, but she shook her head.

"You can choose," she said. "Either you can have it, in which case you won't see me anymore, no matter what it says. Or I tear it up right now into a thousand pieces."

Curious, the human mind. Can think all sorts of things at the same time. No book I ever read had prepared me for this, I thought, and simultaneously it occurred to me that this was the sort of nonsense real people concern themselves with, and then I remembered that Horace had composed wonderful poems on such banal themes, and in the midst of all this I was thinking that I did not want to lose her, and by then I had said go ahead, tear it up, and she had done so. On the paper snowflakes fluttering down I saw torn words, ragged letters, sentences addressed to me now scattered on the floor, impotent and speechless.

"I must go. My things are still in 5B."

The corridors were deserted, our footsteps echoing unrhythmically. On the blackboard in 5B there was a strange diagram, a sort of river system with clotted islands between the streams. I could hear her turning the key in the lock. Little circles floated on the surface of the wide rivers.

"What's this?"

"Lymphatic fluid, capillaries, lymphatic vessels, blood plasma, all the stuff you've got inside you which circulates, and which I don't want to discuss right now."

She was hugging me from behind, her chin resting on my left shoulder, a blur of red in the corner of my eye.

"Let's go to my house," I said, or perhaps implored, for approaching footsteps could be heard in the corridor. We stood very still, clinging to each other. She had kissed me on my glasses, so that I was temporarily sightless, and I could hear the door handle being moved up and down and then released, so that it clicked back into its original position. Then the sound of footsteps again, until they died away.

"We'll go to your house later," she said, "and then I'll stay." So that decision had been taken. We would talk the whole night long, she would take the earliest train, she would go and tell Herfst that she was leaving him, she would move in with me the next evening. She wasn't suggesting, she was letting me know. The following morning I saw her standing by my window staring into the pale early light. I heard what she said.

"I can't stand daylight."

And then she had repeated it, as if she already knew what sort of day this would be, "I can't stand daylight."

And later? She had taken a shower, called out

94

that she didn't want coffee, swept through the room like a whirlwind (Bat having sought refuge under the blankets). I had watched as the red hair strode away from me along the canal. I tried to imagine what it would be like if she were there always, and I could not. Then I sat down to prepare my first lesson of the day: Cicero's *De amicitia,* chapter XXVII, paragraph 104, the lesson I would never give. And I could not concentrate. I extracted the Latin sentence from the edifice of its composition, switched tenses around ("Ladies and gentlemen, I will offer it to you in digestible mouthfuls, since you are so bogged down in your own syntax") but it was no good, I could not. I was in the train with her, and after an hour it was my time to leave, too. Everything looked different, the railing of the bridge over the canal, the staircase in the Central Station, the meadows along the railway line; they all at once struck me as aggressively self-possessed, the most pedestrian details spoke volumes, the world of objects was out to get me. So I was forewarned when I entered the staff room. The first person I saw was Arend Herfst; it was I he was waiting for. Before I could get out the door again he was at my side. He smelled of liquor and hadn't shaved—it seems these things always have to take the same pattern. Next comes the grappling, the scuffling, the yanking at clothes, the raising of voices. Then someone is supposed to intervene, to separate the adversaries, to stand between them. That someone didn't come.

"Herman Mussert, you and I must talk. I have a lot to say to you."

"Not now, later, I've got a lesson."

"I don't care a damn about your lesson, you're staying here."

Not a very common sight—one teacher in hot pursuit of another. I made it to my classroom, tried to enter with composure, but he dragged me out. I broke free and fled into the playground. This was a brilliant move from the point of view of grand spectacle, because now the entire school could watch me being beaten up. I was thrown around the ring—isn't that the expression? As usual I found myself doing all sorts of things at the same time, falling, scrambling to my feet, bleeding, returning a few half-hearted blows, registering the hoarse cries coming from that gaping calf's head, until I couldn't see that either, because he had knocked off my glasses. I groped around in the air until the familiar object was pressed into my hand.

"Your glasses, you prick."

When I put them on again, everything had changed. I could see the white faces of the pupils, masks of furtive mirth, crowded behind the windows. And it was indeed quite a sight: a big stone chessboard with five figures, two of them standing still; as the headmaster strode toward me, Maria Zeinstra was approaching Arend Herfst, who in turn was moving toward Lisa d'India. Just as the headmaster reached me, Herfst pushed Maria Zeinstra out of his way with such force that she stumbled. Before she had time to straighten up again, the headmaster had already said, "Mr. Mussert, you have made your position quite untenable here," but at the same time Herfst had grabbed hold of d'India's arm and was pulling her away.

"Arend!"

It was the same voice that had told me, that very morning, that she wanted to come and live with me. Now everything stood still. I was raised up above that frozen scene, and from above I surveyed the tableau, as if I had no part in it: the older man, his face contorted with anger, shaking his finger at the bleeding figure up against the wall, the red-haired woman in a central position, the other character unsteady on his feet with the girl pinned to his side in an iron grip. The silence was broken by that idiotic name my pupils always called me.

"Socrates."

There was a certain urgency about the word now. Plaintive, refusing to vanish from that playground, it was still lingering there long after it had been exclaimed, spoken or whispered by the voice whose owner had gone, bundled into a car which would collide with a truck a few kilometers away. And no, I did not attend the funeral, and yes, of course Herfst had only broken his legs. And no, I never heard from Maria Zeinstra again, and, indeed, Herfst and I were both fired, and Mr. and Mrs. Arend Herfst now had teaching jobs in Austin,

Texas. No, I never taught again, and yes, I became the author of Dr. Strabo's popular *Travel Guides,* which so many Dutchmen find indispensable on their intrepid foreign sorties. Once in a while I run into a former pupil. A horrifying maturity has always taken possession of their faces; they never utter the two names wafting overhead. Nor do I.

Peter Harris came over to me.

"I thought you couldn't stand the light of day," I said. He smelled of liquor, as Arend Herfst had smelled that morning. The world is a never-ending cross-reference. But at least he wasn't raising his arm to hit me. He held out his flask, and I declined.

"We're getting close to land," he said.

I studied the horizon, but could see nothing.

"Not there; look down here." He indicated the water. It had been gray during the entire voyage, or blue, or black, or all of them at once. Now it was brown.

"Mud from the Amazon. Silt."

"How do you know?"

"I've been here before. And we've been sailing in a southwesterly direction. In a few hours we will see Belém. I have always admired the Portuguese for this—you depart from Belém, you arrive in Belém. There's something cyclical about it, something of eternal recurrence. Not that you believe in that sort of thing, or do you?"

"Only in the case of animals." I was just making conversation.

"Why?"

"Because they always return as themselves. You wouldn't know the difference between a pigeon from 1253 and a present-day pigeon. They're the same pigeons. Either they are immortal, or they keep coming back."

Belém. I could see it clearly. The Praça da República in the sweltering heat, the Paz theater. Some people are fated to have been everywhere before. The university, the zoo with anacondas, gold hares and manatees, the eighteenth-century cathedral. All in Dr. Strabo's *Travel Guide*. Yes, I knew Belém. The Bosque, with its tropical plants, "admission fourteen U.S. Dollar cents." Indian whores. The Goeldi Museum. Don't tell me about the world. My suitcase is my best friend.

The water turned a deeper, more disturbing shade of brown. Large pieces of wood floated on the surface. This was the throat of the great river, this was where the continent spat out its gut; this mud had been carried down from the Andes, through the wounded jungle guarding its last secrets, its last hidden dwellers, the lost world of eternal shadows, the *tenebrae. Procul recedant somnia, et noctium fantasmata.* Protect me from bad dreams, the phantasms of the night. That is the monk's prayer before he goes to sleep. A veil of moisture seemed to hang over the water. In a moment we would set eyes on the two hopelessly distant riverbanks, two lovers who would never embrace. The others, too, had appeared on deck. The woman with the boy, the two old men who looked like twins, the airline pilot with his telescope, everyone in his own niche, alone or in pairs. My traveling companions.

The ocean's sway receded, the steaming sheet of water became a sacrificial dish bearing the ship. Were we still moving at all? I looked at the others, my rare friends whom I had not chosen. We were each other's chance cortège; I belonged with them as they belonged with me. Not for much longer, however. "Gold and timber," I heard Harris say. For a moment his face was obscured by chestnut-brown hair, and I was looking at a featureless man who went on talking as if nothing was the matter. I was beginning to get used to it, these sudden absences, empty contours, hands which you knew were there without actually seeing them. Gold and timber. I was listening; the world still had plenty to say to me, and evidently intended to continue doing so for the time being. Gold—he had written a book about it long ago, this shade of Harris, about the gold war which had raged between Johnson and de Gaulle and which people hadn't talked about because Vietnam had sucked away all the world's attention. And yet it had been a real war, without soldiers but with victims. He had written this book, and no one had read it. And timber, that was why he had come here, to Amazonia. *The Lost World*—had I ever read that book by Conan Doyle; there was a ship in it sailing up the Amazon, too, the *Esmeralda?* Gold and timber, he knew all about them. The gold would stay and the timber would go. "If you come back here in a hundred years' time, you'll find one vast desert, worse than the Sahel. That will be the true end of the world, a depleted morass, a petrified sandpit."

He went on talking, but I must be a past master at levitation, because underneath me the ship sailed on, a tiny craft on the vast expanse of water. It traced a simple V shape behind it, a wedge becoming steadily wider. A page with one solitary letter, which had been trying to tell me something during the entire voyage. But what? I saw the distant shores as two outstretched arms which might well lock the ship in their embrace forever. I saw myself, I saw the summary constellation formed by my traveling companions, three twins, one alone, and I saw how the woman detached herself from the boy and moved in her own path independently of the others, but also how she exerted a certain attraction on us all, as if it were a law of nature, how the two ancients gravitated toward her almost in dance rhythm, how the captain lowered his telescope and followed suit, how Harris detached himself from me, how I, my other self, slowly, hesitantly, joined the group while I rose to ever greater heights like a balloon up above, and saw how the river was superseded by land, more and more land, green, perilous, sweating land, shrouded in its own heat haze which was now melting into the darkness of sudden tropical nightfall. I saw the lights of Belém, as the *Voyager* had seen the earth among all the other asteroids and nebulae of our solar system. Now I had soared higher than Socrates had ever imagined, he who still thought that if only you could rise high enough you would find Heaven. I was higher now than Armstrong, who had tainted the moon. I had to flee from this sidereal cold, I had to return to my place, to my strange body. I was the last to enter the lounge. Alonso Carnero was sitting at the woman's feet. There was something about the ensemble that told me he was to be the center of attention. The two old men looked at him benignly; that was the word. Our bodies seemed undecided as to whether they really wanted to be there; I had seldom seen a group of people with so much missing; every now and again entire knees, shoulders, feet disappeared from view, but our eyes were not in the least disconcerted; they filled in whatever was missing whenever things got too bad, sought out the eyes of the others, as if thereby to exorcise the threat of wholesale disappearance. Only she remained as herself, the boy looked at her and continued to look at her as he spoke. She must have given him some sign to begin.

Begin? That was not the right word, and it is important now to choose the right words; you know that better than I do. He did not begin; he ended.

How can I put it? His story was a story with a beginning and an end, but at the same time it was the end of a story we had already heard quite a lot of—his grandmother shot by the Fascists in Burgos, together with other women from their village, his best friend's grandfather a member of the firing squad; how everyone in the village knew about it and also knew that the women had lifted their skirts at the very last moment of their lives by way of a deadly insult to the soldiers about to shoot; how his parents had forbidden him to play with his friend because such things must never be forgotten, not where he came from, so that he and his friend, whose name was Manolo, used to meet in secret and had in fact been together on the evening about which he would tell us, told us in a litany, a long outpouring of words, describing how he used to challenge Manolo, as Manolo challenged him, and they kept outdoing each other, and they had often lain down on the railway track at night waiting for the Burgos-Madrid express train, just to find out which of them was the bravest. It was very quiet in the lounge; we all saw him getting to his feet and looking like Jesus in the Temple, we knew what was going to happen and we didn't want to hear it, we looked at each other because the sight of him was almost unbearable. His eyes never left her, and I saw something that I would see again when I heard the stories of the others: there was something about the woman that struck a chord of deep familiarity in him, as if she were not who she seemed to be but someone he had known for a very long time, so that he was not telling his story to a stranger but to someone whom only *he* could see. So in fact, while we saw no one but her, the narrator saw someone who inspired him to find the words to express the inner reality of his story.

I heard the ship's engine dying away, and the wide nocturnal river scene ceded to land all around, vast dry plains. They had lain down on the track; he had seen the Great Bear he used to shoot at with his catapult, and he remembered thinking that the Bear was looking down at him, that he could see everything. First Manolo and he had talked awhile; each had boasted that he would not be the first to get up, but this time he had been certain that, as far as he was concerned, it was the truth, and then they had fallen silent; there was some rustling of dry grass, every now and then a car in the distance, that was all. And then, from very far away, the sound had come, almost like a song; it surged right out of the hard iron rails into your skull; he could still feel it. Tears had come to his eyes and he had felt ashamed and at the same time he had been thrilled because everything would fall into place, the terrible, reverberating zoom, the silence in which it approached, the stars above the *meseta,* the tears which turned them into blurry, moist dots of light. No one moved. I remember not daring to look at him anymore, because in his voice the deep rumble had given way to an ear-splitting screech; everything had now become that one sound, no one could ever imagine what it had been like, and as he said that he covered his ears with his hands, and above the noise of what to him must have been a deafening, all-enveloping storm his infinitely soft voice continued, and he described how he had seen Manolo scrambling to his feet just as the gigantic, black, heavy mass had come over him, Alonso; and with his arms outstretched as if he wanted to illustrate how a body is torn in two, he stood in the middle of the lounge and looked around without seeing any of us, and we, we did not move and saw how she got up and led him outside with a gesture of infinite tenderness.

We sat there for some time, and then went up on deck. No one spoke. I stood at the stern and looked at the southern bank, where the distant sounds were coming from. I saw nothing, only the reflection of our lights on the satin water. So this was how it was. The world would continue to enact its masques of day and night as if to remind us of something, and we, who were already elsewhere, would observe this. I knew the country that was invisible to us now, I knew what was going on there, on those distant shores. We would sail through the Narrows, a labyrinth of muddy yellow waterways, the trees of the great forest within touching distance; in the Furo Grande our ship would brush against the branches. I knew it all, I had been here before. Of course I had. Naked Indian children on rafts, huts on stilts in the water, dugouts with hieroglyphic oarsmen, the shrieking and chattering of troops of monkeys in the tree canopy when night falls. Falls *again*. Occasionally an electrical storm scrawls its livid, lightning alphabets, illegible, flickering in the black sky. Having left the Narrows behind us, the flat-topped mountains loom like strange tables, and then Santarém, halfway to Manaos, with its insane opera house, the green water of the Tapajós merging with the gilded mud, and the other, so much more brilliant green and red and yellow of the screeching parrots, the butterflies like floating brightly colored snippets of cloth, and in the evening the hand-sized velvet moths scorching their wings on the deck lights. That was how it must go on, a heaviness, a burden, and we the travelers in limbo.

Every evening, if that was the right word, one of us would tell his story, and I would know them and not know them, and each of those stories would be the end of another, longer story. The only thing was, the others seemed to know so much better than I what story to tell. Yes, I know now, but I didn't know then. The teller of a story without end is a poor storyteller, as you well knew. No one was afraid, as far as I could see. We were past that stage. What I myself felt was an elation that I could not explain.

The river became narrower, but was still as wide as a lake. At Manaos we crossed the line dividing the Amazon and the Rio Negro, the black water flowing side by side with the brown in midstream, two shades defying integration, the black water of death polished like onyx, the brown tanned and tough, telling of distance, of jungle. When it would be my turn I did not know; for the time being I was content to listen to the others and watch, to read the anecdotes of their lives as if they had been invented especially for me. The priest listened to Harris's story as if he were hearing confession once more, while Harris himself did not have to hear Father Fermi's story because he had already gone by then. He was the second in line, and we listened to him as we would listen to all the rest; it was a ceremony of parting, a celebration of the coincidence that had attached our lives to a time and a place and a name. And we were courteous, we died each other's deaths, we helped each other to stretch that final second to last until the end of each story; there was still work to be done, there was thinking to be done, and there seemed to be no end to the time we had for this purpose. Harris had been knifed in a bar in Guyana, all those interminable seconds during which the flashing silver blade was piercing his body he had had the time to embark in Lisbon and to travel with us and still that fatal stab had not come to an end. There had been some trouble about a black woman at a shabby brothel in a suburb of Georgetown, from a distance of two thousand kilometers he had seen the jealous knife coming toward him, he had been able to store his entire life in that instant, he had been struck by how *logically*—that was the word he had used—his life had taken its course.

Thirteen minutes—of course Captain Dekobra still remembered precisely—had elapsed between the moment that the first of his four engines had failed and the moment he touched the surface of the sea. *Sound of impact.* He told us about the cloud in the cloudless sky, which, because the sun had been behind him, had looked like the gigantic silver figure of a man who seemed to fill the whole sky as he approached. He had not at that particular moment thought of the hundreds of pilgrims who had left Mecca with him on his chartered flight, but of his wife in Paris and his girlfriend in Djakarta, but most of all he had thought of two banal containers lying in their separate freezers somewhere down below. All the rest had meanwhile continued: the radar had not been working properly once again: it had taken him a while to realize that it was a cloud of volcanic ash rising from the crater of Krakatau beneath him; he had heard his engines dying on him, one by one; the temperature dropped from 350 degrees to nothing for lack of combustion; naturally he had been scared, he had tried to restart the engines with the backup ignition, but there was no reaction, no propulsion, and suddenly it had felt just like his first flight in a glider, so long ago, only this was the biggest glider the world had ever seen.

With an unearthly swishing sound they had planed through the air; he had heard shouts coming from behind him, he had fallen back on his emergency batteries, he had sent out his Mayday signal, and in the midst of all that feverish activity an unearthly calm had come over him. It had, he said, lasted a year, long enough for him to have written his memoirs, his recollections of the war, the battles in the sky, the bombings, the two women in his life for whom he always prepared a special meal before his departure, which he left in their freezers so that they would eat them when he was on the other side of the world; it was ridiculous and childish maybe, but it had always been a source of surreptitious pleasure. Just as it gave him pleasure now to imagine that later, when he was gone, those two women who were oblivious to each other's existence would eat a meal that had actually been prepared by him, who was no longer of this world, and didn't we find this amusing, and sure enough we found it amusing and looked into his steely blue eyes, and that's how he, too, left us, straight-backed, with a spring in his step, a man who was unafraid, who had sailed through the air in one of the world's biggest aircraft like a folded paper dart; he took the hand you extended. I saw the two of you disappear through the glass doors of the lounge.

That night was the last time I dreamed of myself in bed in Amsterdam, but I, the man in the bed, was beginning to bore me. The perspiration on his brow, those contorted features, the expression saying that there was a lot of suffering going on even though I was sailing peacefully up the Amazon all the while, the alarm clock next to my bed in which time seemed to have been bonded with glue and me having been through so much in the meantime. I thought he should get on with it: the suffering there, on his face, had nothing to do with the sensation of apotheosis of me, here. There were only three of us left now, and for someone in whom the classics have instilled the idea that stories should have a beginning and an end, things were not looking too good. I could not make a crash landing, no one had ever stuck a knife in me, indeed the only time I had been confronted with physical violence was on that one occasion when Arend Herfst had beaten me up, and even then he had exercised restraint.

Father Fermi was beset by no such problems. He told us quite candidly about the joy he had felt upon receiving his abbot's permission to make the pilgrimage to Santiago de Compostela. He had had a vivid picture in his mind: the pillar at the entrance to the cathedral, where for centuries now pilgrims had rested their hands in relief upon completion of their arduous journey, so that a whole hand had been eroded in the polished marble. It was a strong image, I must admit he made much more of it than I had done in Dr. Strabo's *Guide to Western and Northern Spain*. I had mentioned it, no more, but he turned it into high drama: how it was possible that a hand leaned against a marble pillar should lift off a tiny particle of marble, a microscopic fragment, invisible to the naked eye, and how all those hands across all those centuries had, as a result of that one gesture repeated over and over, sculpted a hand that was *not there*. How long would it take if one had to do that on one's own? Twenty centuries, perhaps! I knew what he was talking about, for I myself had been one of the sculptors, I, too, had rested my hand in that absent hand. Dom Fermi, however, had never done so. When he arrived at Santiago from Milan after walking for three months, he had done what everyone did (recommended by Dr. Strabo): he had climbed to the top of Monte Gozo to view the silhouette of the cathedral in the distance, he had gone down on his knees and prayed, and then he had rushed down the hillside in ecstasy (he said this with some embarrassment) and at the bottom, when he was crossing the street to walk "on the right side," he had been knocked down by an ambulance. Just as he had acted out his pilgrimage for us, an old man with dancing steps, so he now danced himself over backward under the weight of that ambulance, flailing his arms as if an immense bird had flown at him, or a terrifying angel. Professor Deng had to jump up to steady him, but he didn't even notice; his eyes were fixed on you alone. What had you conjured up for him to see? None of us will ever know what the other saw when he was telling you his story, but whatever face you show, recognizable or absolutely not, expected or unexpected, it must have something to do with fulfillment. I wonder.

Only Deng is left, and it is his turn now. The ship seems to crawl along, as if reluctant to go any farther. I am aware of the nocturnal jungle surrounding us. When we pass a settlement I can smell dried fish and rotting fruit. Sometimes I hear the voices of children over the water, now and then a boat with Indians passes by, after which the sobbing of the diesel engine takes a while to die away. Coari, Fefé, the world still has names here.

The two of you are already there when I arrive. I will have to tell my story to you alone. You are wearing your Persephone mask (Father Fermi: "But you as a classical scholar ought to know that death is a woman") but Professor Deng sees something else, something that perhaps corresponds to the poet who has been his lifelong companion, just as Ovid has been mine, and suddenly his old man's voice can be heard imitating the crowd heckling him, his own students in the days of the Cultural Revolution. He had been forced to stand on a platform and had been spat upon and beaten for betraying the revolutionary cause, for having indulged in the decadent, feudal pastimes of the exploiting class by glorifying a caste that had humiliated the people, and for devoting himself to the superstitions and irrelevant private emotions of men from a contemptible past. He had been lucky, for he had survived. He was banished to a remote corner of the countryside, where he stayed until new changes announced themselves, but something had snapped inside him. Like Qu Yuan he now felt captive in a diseased era in which he did not wish to live, and then he had seen the wheels of change revolving once more and he had turned his back on the world and fled. He quoted his poet: "I experienced calumny in the morning and expulsion the very same night."

Taking his poem as his only luggage, he had started walking until he reached a river, and thus he had left behind his life, like a discarded object on the shore. The water had weighed down his clothes; he had floated like a little boat and had waited for the wind to rise so that he could embark on his great voyage. Around him he had heard the water murmuring in all sorts of voices, very soft and gentle it had sounded. He gestured to you with his arm, he had almost vanished already, as if he were made of a delicate, immensely old material, and you had made the same gesture and had already got to your feet. In the distant mirror of the lounge I saw myself sitting alone and thought of that man in Amsterdam, the photograph in his hand, the dream he dreamed of me thinking of him. I made my way past that Socrates to the door, I looked into the blind eyes under the gross eyebrows, at the pensive caveman's head filled with thoughts of me in Amsterdam.

The ship left hardly a trace in the water behind it; the river was so still and black that I saw the shimmering snakes and scorpions, the gods and heroes reflected in the dark glass. I would have been quite happy to slip down into the water like Professor Deng, I had seen the euphoria of farewell written on his face. The guttural croaking of toads or giant frogs rose from the banks. How long I stood there I do not know, the sun in the east set the jungle in a terrible blaze once more. Once more the hasty flash of day swept over the river until the blackness unfolded again, enveloping birds and trees, covering everything. The man in Amsterdam had gone to sleep unknowing, ignorant of the voyage that lay in store for him. Someone would find him as soon as I told you my story. People would come to lay out that stocky body, to burn it in the crematorium at Driehuis-Westerveld. My impossible family would throw away my Ovid translation, or, God knows, would burn it as well; Dr. Strabo's *Travel Guides* would remain in print for the next ten years or so, until they found some other fool to write them, a former pupil would read the announcement of Herman Mussert's death and say, "Hey, Socrates is dead," and at the same time I would change. It was not my soul that would set out on a journey, as the real Socrates had imagined; it was my body that would embark on endless wanderings, never to be ousted from the universe, and so it would take part in the most fantastic metamorphoses, about which it would tell me nothing because it would long since have forgotten all about me. At one time the matter it had consisted of had housed a soul that resembled me, but now my matter would have other duties. And I? I had to turn around, I had to let go of the ship's rail, to let go of everything, to look at you. You beckoned; it was not difficult to follow. You had taught me something about infinity, about how an immeasurable space of memories can be stored in the most minute time span, and while I was permitted to remain as small and coincidental as I was, you had shown me my true stature. You needn't beckon me any longer, I'm coming. None of the others will hear my story, none of them will see that the woman sitting there waiting for me has the features of my dearest Crito, the girl who was my pupil, so young that one could speak about immortality with her. And then I told her, then I told you

the following story

# HARVEST IN TRANSLATION

Stanislaw Benski   *Missing Pieces*

Umberto Eco   *The Name of the Rose*

Bohumil Hrabal   *Too Loud a Solitude*

Pawel Huelle   *Who Was David Weiser?*
*Moving House*

Danilo Kiš   *Garden, Ashes*

Pavel Kohout   *I Am Snowing: The Confessions*
*of a Woman of Prague*

George Konrád   *A Feast in the Garden*

Cees Nooteboom   *The Following Story*

Amos Oz   *Fima*
*In the Land of Israel*
*A Perfect Peace*
*To Know a Woman*

Octavio Paz   *The Other Voice: Essays*
*on Modern Poetry*

José Saramago   *The Gospel According to Jesus Christ*
*The Year of the Death of Ricardo Reis*

Luis Sepúlveda   *The Old Man Who Read Love Stories*

A. B. Yehoshua   *A Late Divorce*
*The Lover*
*Mr. Mani*